Sasquatch 6

THE FORGOTTEN OZARK FOREST DEVILS

Jeffrey B Miley

Pastor Jeff Mysteries Series

Wolves Among the Sheep

Revenge In The Woods Series:

Shriek.   Shriek 2-Cain's Revenge.   Shriek 3-3.   Shriek 4-The Chair.   Shriek 5-The Witch Is Back
Shriek 6-The Conclusion: Come Hell or High Water

Sasquatch Adventures Series:

Sasquatch-The Cave

Sasquatch 2: The Mask

Sasquatch 3: The Troop

Sasquatch 4: The Clone

Sasquatch 5: The Pioneers

Sasquatch 6: The Forgotten Ozark Forest Devils

Sasquatch 7: The Slot Canyon

Sasquatch 8: The Anthology

Sasquatch 9: Yeti of the Spin Ghar: Blood in the Snow

Sasquatch 10: MoMo: The Fort Leavenworth Encounters

Sasquatch 11: Anthology 2

Sasquatch 12: The Change

Sasquatch 13: The Forest Sentinel

Sasquatch 14: Alone: In Ape Canyon

Sasquatch 15: The Unlost Child

Sasquatch 16: Tcinto Saktco: Sasquatch Killer

Sasquatch 17: Circus

Sasquatch 18: Issa

Sasquatch 19: The Boys

Sasquatch 20: The Rest Area

Sasquatch 21: Deadly Cargo

Sasquatch 22: The Boys Grow Up

Sasquatch 23: Alone At Boggy Creek

Sasquatch 24: The Church Camp

Sasquatch 25: Bigfoot & Me

Sasquatch 26: Night Terrors

Sasquatch 27: 62

Sasquatch 28: The Town

Sasquatch 29: Bones

Sasquatch 30: HOAX

Sasquatch 31: Rabies: Infection of the Raystown Man

Sasquatch 32: Pet

Sasquatch 33: Albino

Sasquatch 34: Rampage in the Campground

Sasquatch 35: Alone At Willow Creek

Sasquatch 36: Nacogdoches and the Monsters of East Texas

Sasquatch 37: The Alliance

Sasquatch 38: Snow Monster

Sasquatch 39: Fire

Sasquatch 40: Twins

Sasquatch 41: Enemy

Sasquatch 42: Swampus

Sasquatch 43: Imaginary

full blood moon series:

full blood moon

full blood moon 2

full blood moon 3-Winnie's Springs

full blood moon 4-The Carnival

full blood moon 5-The Carnival Revisited: Blood Loss

Other titles:

The Werewolf King.   Death to the Werewolf King.   Werewolf King 3: Grizzly

Abandoned

Struck

Killing the Past

Time Jaunt-Saving Custer

Manny

The Bouncy House

The Church

The Silver Cigar Series-Alien at My Window.   The Silver Cigar Series-Aliens in My Basement

The Whimpering End of the World Series

When the Flesh Grows Cold.   Heartbeats in the Graveyard

Table of Contents

Chapter 1

A Bit of History

In 1686, a trading post in Arkansas was established and was the first settlement in the lower Mississippi Valley. It was established by Henri de Tonti. He was an Italian explorer working with La Salle, the famous French explorer.

The Arkansas Post became an important trading hub and lifeline for the area. It eventually came under Spanish control and then back under French control. It became part of the Louisiana Purchase, but that didn't happen until 1803.

While the Arkansas Post and surrounding stockade changed leadership over the decades, there were two men who chronicled the events that support the existence of the Ozark Forest Devils.

The first was a Frenchman by the name of Jacques De Beaumont. He was the lead trader, accountant and an avid journal writer.

Not only did he keep detailed records of the business transactions during his tenure, he kept historical records of the events that transpired during his seventeen years at the post.

He took on a Quapaw (Algonquin Indian) wife which he gained in a trade for seven beaver pelts and two deer hides. He didn't romanticize the transaction, nor the subsequent years of marriage with the poor woman.

She was basically a slave who cooked, cleaned and suffered being raped by her husband several times a week. Her existence was solely for the pleasure of this somewhat horrible human being.

In a drunken rage over some minor offense, Beaumont beat her to death with a beaver trap. No one in the small settlement batted an eye. She was, after all, just an Indian woman and, therefore, his property. No one cared.

And yet his foul deeds appeared in his journals. The man was a truthful recordkeeper, even when he looked bad himself. Her death haunted him the rest of his life.

Now you know Beaumont's character or lack thereof.

I include him for the five references he made about a band of creatures that terrorized the area near the trading post. Remember, this man was not given to flights of fancy or creative story-telling. He recorded facts.

His first description simply recounted the story of a group of trappers who had been attacked. Three of the beasts had killed two of the six men, and the remaining four had narrowly escaped.

The men described the animals as being seven feet tall, hairy and walking upright like a man. Nothing more.

His second journal entry concerning the creatures is the most interesting. It occurred almost five months after the first incident. Jacques had gone fishing with a group of men, and they were attacked by a single beast.

Several of the men were armed and drove it off, but his description is noteworthy. It is his eyewitness account.

He stated that the beast was eight feet tall, hairy all over, with blood red eyes and small horns on top of its head. This description was repeated in the three subsequent journal entries that he penned.

The additional three entries were the eyewitness accounts of others. He made no claim of ever seeing the monster again.

His journals are part of the permanent pre-Louisiana Purchase archive in the Smithsonian Institute. All items are pre-1804 historic finds from the specific region known as the Louisiana Purchase and include many Spanish, French, British and American memorabilia. The items are currently not on display, nor have they ever been shown to the public. The archive holds over forty-five million documented items.

The next person to journal about the creatures was Juan Alvarez Batista. For almost a decade during the period of

Spanish occupation, he was the Lieutenant in charge of the garrison that called the trading post home.

His journal entries were also a mixture of other eyewitness accounts and his own firsthand sightings.

He penned over eleven entries. The most notable was the entry where Batista and fifteen soldiers went hunting for the beasts after traders were attacked.

After several hours of tracking, the beasts were located. They were looking for only two, but they encountered seven. There was a confrontation and two of the beasts were shot, but not killed. The soldiers didn't fare as well. Three were killed and two were badly injured.

It would have been worse, according to his journal entry, but one of the men, his bugler, blew his instrument in desperation. The beasts had never heard the musical implement before and were frightened off before more casualties were amassed.

Batista's description of the beasts matches Beaumont's depiction to a tee: Red eyes, hairy body and horns on the forehead.

Batista's journals may also be found in the same archive as Beaumont's. Specifically, the items are archived with other items from the Arkansas Trading Post (Ozarks Collection).

From those beginnings and into the modern era of the Civil War, stories have been told and swapped about the forest devils.

In late 1862, the Confederates built a huge earthworks fort named Fort Hindman where the trading post had been. In January of 1863, a three-day battle saw the fort fall.

The Union bombardment overwhelmed the fort and surrounding area. Since that battle had taken place, the number of sightings of the forest devils became almost nonexistent.

There are many hypotheses as to why that would be, including the skeptic's explanation that the creatures never existed. Another theory is that the noise and destruction of the Civil War battle had so traumatized the creatures that avoiding man became a rule of survival for the forest devils.

No matter the reason, the Ozark Forest Devils must not be forgotten They are a part of our cryptozoological record. They are most likely still wandering the hills and valleys of the forty-seven thousand square miles known as the Ozarks.

Chapter 2

The Incursion into Spanish Territory (The Recap)

Major Reginald Smythe led his men across the wilderness from Pennsylvania, the Ohio Valley and the newly formed Indiana Territory. All along the way, they met hale and hardy individuals.

Some were educated and some not, but they were mostly decent folk. Once they entered the Upper Missouri Territory, that all changed. There was no discernable explanation for it. Except, possibly, that there was an odd mixture of French and Spanish in amongst the American settlers.

The people seemed uneducated to a fault. One could say they were very backwards. Many lacked basic manners and morals. He had already encountered two men that were sleeping with their own daughters, having lost their wives to the harsh lifestyle and conditions. There were other inexcusable behaviors as well. He knew that to be effective, he would have to overlook the odd behaviors and stick to his mission.

It was the United States government that was calling the area the Upper Missouri Territory. And the United States had no claim there, even amongst rumors that the area had changed hands from Spanish to French. And there were further rumors that the French were looking to sell their holdings to raise money to fight the British who were half a world away.

The United States didn't care about the current owners or the new owners of the area. The Upper Missouri Territory was populated by Americans. It was guessed that the Spanish territory, or French, depending on whose rumors were most up to date, was almost seventy percent American settlers.

And it was American settlers and pioneers that were coming under attack. Not by Indians, as most would think, but by giants of some sort that were native to the area. Further clarification describe them as inhuman giants.

The offenses were occurring in an area that was becoming known as the Ozarks. The name seemed to be a bastardization of the French term *aux Arkansas*, which meant *of Arkansas* and was shortened to *aux arcs*. There was a nearby outpost established by the French called Arkansas.

Smythe and his men had come to the rescue with two hundred soldiers and three cannons in tow. He had strict orders to avoid contact with French and/or Spanish troops.

The sole mission was to eradicate the animals responsible for bothering the homesteaders. The United States wanted the settlers to stay in place. Having the majority population in this foreign territory gave the United States government the upper hand in negotiations to acquire the territory.

Major Smythe was aware of all the intricacies, diplomatic necessities and rumors concerning his assignment. He was university educated and planned on making the rank of General one day. This assignment was an important step towards that goal.

The settlement to which they were headed was a place called Thornside. It boasted a population of two hundred and thirty-two. It had been two hundred and ninety-five, but the hairy giants had killed fifty-eight of the sixty-three casualties. The other five people died from normal frontier maladies.

One of those killed was the son-in-law of a rich Washington kingmaker, who had been seeking to grab up some land in the volatile area. The Spanish were offering land to Americans in the hopes that the protestant Americans would eventually swear allegiance to France and convert to Catholicism. It wasn't working out well for the Spaniards.

The Washington businessman had requested his son-in-law go to secure some landholdings for their family. The local beasts killed the man, and now the United States Army was involved at the behest of the powerful politician.

Once they arrived at Thornside, Smythe had his main contingent wait outside of the settlement as he and his Lieutenant, along with four soldiers, entered to announce their presence.

After they had passed through the gate, everyone stopped their activities to stare. All the men, and quite a few of the women, were armed. It was the strangest welcome he had ever received. In fact, no one stepped forward to welcome them at all.

He noticed that although the settlement had a gate, an entire section of wall had yet to be built. He made a mental note to address that glaring issue.

The townspeople were sizing them up. Most had never seen the uniform of the American soldiers before. They were wondering whether they were about to run off Spanish soldiers or the ever annoying Frenchies.

Major Smythe spoke to a cluster of citizens at a well near what appeared to be the center of town, "Good morning. I am Major Smythe of the United States Army. Do you have a leader I may speak to?"

The townsfolk stared slack-jawed at the contingent and seemingly unimpressed. After a few uncomfortable moments, an old woman stepped forward. She looked them up and down and then sideways.

"So you pretty boys are United States soldiers?" she asked, as if she had not heard the Major's introduction.

"Yes, Ma'am," Smythe replied.

"I'm Grammy Hillburn. I guess you could say I'm the mayor of this here town, although we ain't never had nobody with that oh-ficial title. I take care of everybody best I can," she stated as a matter of fact.

"A woman? In charge?" Smythe blundered.

The old woman snapped her fingers and every gun was up and pointed at the Major.

Major Smythe was fairly unflappable, "Ma'am, if you shoot me, the two hundred men I have right outside of town will have no choice but to level your little settlement. They will assume you have allied yourself with the Spanish or the French. And then we won't be able to help you end your giant problem."

"Giant problem?" she asked, and then said, "Oh, you mean the forest devils. Is that why you are here?"

"Yes, Grammy Hillburn. That is our mission."

She liked him. He showed no fear when every musket was trained on him. She raised her arms and bounced them up and down with her palms down, giving her men the all clear sign.

The muskets were lowered. One of them accidentally fired and ricocheted off the hard-packed dirt and rock of the street, just missing Widow Sumner.

"Asshole!" the widow yelled.

Grammy shook her head and said, "Clarence, keep your damn finger off'n the trigger until you're ready to shoot!" She looked up at Smythe and said, "You shoulda been a little more nervous with assholes like that pointing a gun at ya."

He liked her too. She was funny and honest. A great combination where he was concerned.

"So you wanna see one?" the old woman asked.

For a moment, he was in a fog and didn't comprehend what she was asking, and then it hit him. She had a dead forest devil for him to look at.

"Please, Grammy. Show us." He got down off his horse, as did the Lieutenant. They handed their reigns to the enlisted men and followed their hostess.

"We just caught him yesterday. We baited him with a calf, and he fell into our hole. We think he broke his leg." She walked around twenty more yards, and then she pointed at a large hole which had been dug.

The pit, obviously, had taken quite a bit of time to create. It was about twelve feet by twelve feet.

Smythe looked over the edge and couldn't believe what he was looking at. The pit was between twelve and fifteen feet deep. The creature looked to be about seven to eight feet tall.

It roared and growled. As it moved around, it favored its right leg. It looked up into Smythe's eyes and snarled. The Major had the sudden urge to urinate.

The beast was covered in hair except its face. Its eyes were eerily human but red. The Major had seen an albino rabbit once. Its red eyes were not the least unnerving. But this beast's eyes looked inside of you with hate and disdain.

Its canine teeth appeared longer than expected for something so human-looking, and it had two nubs on either side of its forehead. He wondered what they were.

As if Grammy knew what he was thinking, she said, "Those bumps is horns. This is a young'un. The full growed adult's horns break through the skin. They only git maybe two inches long, but if one of 'em butts you with it, it feels much longer. Them horns is why we call 'em forest devils. Oh, and them damn red eyes. I imagine Beelzebub himself ain't got eyes scarier than that."

Just then a young boy threw a rock and hit the beast in the face. The forest devil bent down, picked it up and threw it back, solidly plinking the kid on the forehead with such force that it knocked him backward.

"And unfortunately, Major, they can do that. And with much larger rocks. They've killed and injured quite a few of us that way. And I ain't sure why, but I think they are pretty smart."

Grammy went over and roughly pulled the boy to his feet and said, "Do that again Enoch, and I'll throw you in with him!"

The boy, looking ready to piss himself, broke loose and ran off.

"So, Grammy, what are you going to do with this one?"

"It's bait. They'll come for it. And when they do, we'll kill a few, at least. Of course, with you and your men here now, maybe we can get them all," she answered.

"And how many would you guess there are?" Smythe prodded.

"We counted fifteen once. Since then we killed one and now this one. There may be more though. We have no way of knowing," she answered honestly.

"Lieutenant," Smythe began, "I want a detachment lying in wait tonight. Let's jump right in and kill a few."

Lieutenant Elliott smiled and said, "Yessir. I'll ride out immediately."

Elliott turned, mounted his horse and hurried off.

"Is there anything else you would like to show me?" the Major asked Grammy.

"Let me show you the graveyard," she said.

"And what is there that may be of interest to me, my good woman?"

She cackled at the good woman remark. She hadn't been a good woman for years.

She looked him in the eye and said, "Just thought you'd like to see where you can bury your men, when the time comes."

Chapter 3

Major Reginald Smythe

Major Reginal Smythe had a plan. He wished to be a career soldier and retire from serving his country as a General.

As a Lieutenant, he served with distinction as an Indian fighter in Western Pennsylvania and the Ohio Valley. In 1794 at the Battle of Fallen Timbers near the southwestern shore of Lake Erie, he was wounded twice while saving others.

He found that killing Indians was something he was disinclined to enjoy, as many officers did. It was not lost on the young Lieutenant that this had always been their country, and the white settlers were stealing their land.

It was pointed out to him, on more than one occasion, that the Indians had begun the hostilities years ago. If they had just agreed to share this beautiful country, there would be no problems.

That always made him laugh. Never had he heard, in the history of the world, that anyone shared their country with an invading force. Yet many of his contemporaries believed this to be truth.

As much as he hated rousting the Indians from their rightful land, he was a good soldier. He wished to make the military a career and serve this great new nation. And maybe along the way, he could help the Indians preserve their land and heritage, if the opportunities arose.

To that end, he returned east where he dated and then married a young woman. Her father was Oscar Pendleton, a successful merchant. His name was well-known in Washington.

The man and his great wealth had already helped to seat a senator from Pennsylvania and two congressmen, one from New York and the other from New Jersey.

He felt it would be good to have such a powerful man as a father-in-law. And Reginald was correct. After marrying Pendleton's daughter, Katherine, he went from Lieutenant to Captain in two months. In just six short months, he was promoted to Major. His career was advancing just as he had hoped.

But as with any of life's endeavors, there can be drawbacks and pitfalls. His was Katherine.

On the surface, he was a lucky man. She was both beautiful and had a rich family. Reggie was the envy of his peers. What could possibly go wrong?

Katherine was indeed a sight to behold, but the woman was as frigid as the Arctic. On their honeymoon night, he literally wrestled the woman and then, for lack of a better term, raped her, so they could consummate the union.

She, of course, was traumatized and complained to her mother the next day. She had not been properly prepared for some of life's realities.

"Momma, he held me down and thrust himself inside me, like a beast!" she cried.

As a young woman, mother had no great education on the matter either.

"Well, dear, those things happen. You must endure it from time to time. It is what a good wife does. It is a requirement," Mrs. Pendleton instructed her daughter.

"Then I don't wish to be a good wife! Or a wife at all, for that matter!" Katherine declared.

"Don't be silly, sweetheart. You are a grown woman, and you have found yourself a good man. Now deal with it maturely, and you will find yourself the wife of a General one day. You mark my words," Mrs. Pendleton promised.

Katherine was unimpressed.

Over the next six months, things did not improve. All of Reginald's acts of intimacy were met with rebuff, even obtaining a kiss from her was a task.

Reggie had enough of this selfish, self-involved, self-centered child that he had married. Shortly after being promoted to Major, he began an affair with a woman below his station, and he couldn't have been happier.

Unfortunately, Oscar Pendleton had eyes and ears everywhere. He discovered his son-in-law's infidelity and called him on it.

Reggie didn't mince words, and he told Mr. Pendleton exactly what was happening.

Oscar replied, "Oh, that. Her mother is the same way. Every time I touch the woman, she stiffens up, straight as a board."

"So what do you do for physical, uh, release?" Reggie asked.

"The same thing you did. But I can't have you doing that to my daughter, right under her nose," Oscar said.

"She doesn't care, sir," Smythe replied. ·

"But if you are found out, then we all look bad. So I am going to send you out West. Gene Tierney just lost his son-in-law in a mishap out in the Spanish lands. Other Americans are at risk as well. You'll lead the expedition and take your young woman as a camp follower. Nobody will be the wiser," Pendleton explained. "You'll get your orders in the morning."

"The Army is okay with this?" Reggie asked.

"Gene Tierney owns more politicians than I do. It was already decided. They just needed a good leader to take an entire battalion out there," the older man explained.

And so it came to be. Katherine kissed him on the cheek as he left. He could be gone over a year, and she had no reaction, except to be relieved he wouldn't be around trying to be her husband. That was when he knew that he hated her.

He asked Constance to follow his battalion. Usually a group of women, as many as thirty-five or forty, would follow a military unit. They would wash cloths, mend uniforms, help with the cook's duties and provide sexual favors to the troops.

She said yes, but stated that she wouldn't service the other men, only him. He agreed.

As he stood in that cemetery with Grammy Hillburn, he thought of how much more rewarding it was to be here facing monsters, than to be back in polite society while being married to Katherine. She was a different kind of monster. The kind that empties a man's soul.

At least he and his men could shoot at these monsters. He had no clue how to get rid of Katherine Smythe when he returned home.

What Major Reginald Smythe had just led across this great nation was two hundred and four men, a fifteen-mule supply train, three chuck wagons, four supply wagons that were pulled by mules, three cannons and three caissons pulled by six horses. Thirty-two women accompanied the battalion to take care of the most basic needs of his unit.

Along the way, two men had deserted and two had died from illness. One of the women had perished from complications in childbirth. No one had known that she was pregnant. She was a large girl from the start. Had her pregnancy been known, she would have not been allowed to accompany them.

The baby survived and was passed between the remaining women who cared for the little girl. She had thirty-one aunts who all loved her.

Constance became especially attached to her. This caused Reggie no small amount of concern. But he was happy for the child.

His greatest hope was that they could find a decent family here in Thornside. At first blush, that didn't seem too likely.

The Major and his command had moved forward for seventy-six days. Weather had not cooperated with them at many spots along the way. Flooding and river fording had caused a few complications.

All in all, Reggie was pleased at their success and low mortality rate. Now he stood in a cemetery that the old woman had all but guaranteed he would be needing.

Chapter 4

Grammy Hillburn

Grammy Hillburn was so much more than anyone knew. Everyone knew she was smart. She was kind, with just enough pepper in her temperament to get her point across. Grammy was compassionate to a fault.

But no one had known that Grammy had been a nurse and a midwife. At times, she had been the only medical professional in whatever town that she was currently living.

She had delivered babies, set broken limbs and even removed musket balls when they weren't too near the spine or major organs. She had more medical knowledge and experience than most doctors beyond the eastern seaboard.

She had one weakness: Her heart.

Grammy had a history of meeting and falling in love with married men, but not doctors. Although, had there been any doctors around to choose from, maybe so.

Her weakness was for ruggedly handsome leaders along the new and wild edge of America. She liked take-charge men, but they usually married gutless women with little backbone.

When one of those take-charge men met her, they had met their match. Although she rarely drank alcohol, she could cuss and play cards as good as any man. And she could hold her own in any conversation.

She had grown up on a farm, fought off Indians, fought off randy suitors, sought out education and was eventually able to secure an apprenticeship with Doctor G.B. Denton in Lancaster, Pennsylvania.

Apprenticing under Denton for over seven years, she then headed west with a group of settlers that were headed to the Fort Dearborn area.

Grammy settled for short periods of time in many villages and settlements in that area. She always found herself greatly appreciated until her predilection for married men would kick in.

She was driven out of at least three villages, and the last time, she was pregnant. That was when she met a kind and lonely man named Thomas Hillburn.

He took pity on her and she on him. They were married. Priscilla Dugan, Grammy's maiden name, was a good and faithful wife. Grammy was also an excellent mother.

She did not love her husband in a romantic way, but he loved her and that was enough for almost twenty years. Her first child, to another man, was Lilly Dugan Hillburn. Their union produced three more children, all girls.

In their nineteenth year of marriage, Thomas suffered a debilitating stroke and died two months later. Grammy nursed him the best that she could. Although she didn't love him, she respected him and was grateful for his infinite kindness. She was sorry to see him pass.

Grammy began nursing again, to support herself and her daughters. Life on the frontier was hard. She still had the Hillburn homestead, and that was a blessing.

She did her best to avoid married men and concentrated on raising her girls. Her youngest daughter, Samantha, died from complications from scarlet fever at age nine, shortly after Thomas had passed.

Lilly and her remaining sisters, Beth and Laura, grew up and married fine men and began having babies of their own. It was during that period when she was dubbed Grammy.

The name stuck fast, and even when she called on homes needing her nursing skills, she was greeted as Grammy.

The truth was that Grammy was a handsome woman and had an attractiveness about her. But she didn't fall into the category of pretty or beautiful by any means. And she certainly didn't fall into the dew-kissed flower category that the name Priscilla brought to mind.

Grammy fit her like a glove. She was a wonderful grandmother, nurturing and supportive. Truth be told, she hated the name because it made her sound too matronly, and she was still hoping to find love again. And she did.

At age of fifty-one, she found a man in the next village over. He was just her type. He had broken his leg, and she was called to set it. It was love at first sight for both.

But as it always happened for her, the man's wife took offense and threatened to expose her if she didn't leave the area. Not wanting to bring shame down upon her daughters or grandchildren, she lied to them and told them she was asked to join a wagon train going into the Spanish Louisiana Territory.

She did go with that wagon train, but she hadn't been asked. Nevertheless, she quickly became a valuable member of the group, plying her medical skills. And she, even as a single woman, was eligible for a homestead being offered by the Spanish.

The wagon master, Charles Danby, was killed during a Quapaw Indian attack. The assistant wagon master, Harrison Stillman, took over. He was a fairly capable leader.

Shortly after they reached their destination, Stillman began to show signs of consumption. As a lifelong pipe smoker, he had set the wheels in motion of his own demise.

Three months after their arrival, he died. It was shortly before the first forest devil attack. Grammy had nursed the man and made his last days as comfortable as possible, which included letting him smoke two pipes a day.

She knew it interfered with his breathing a bit, but she didn't figure it would hasten his death. That conclusion was already established as the weight just fell off the man. At the end, he was a pitiful skeleton, lying in his bed.

The man that took over was Bertram Lohr. He was a good man, but he was more about socializing and glad-handing than running the serious business of establishing a settlement in the Louisiana Territory.

Under Bert, many things went undone. A stockade was supposed to be erected around the buildings that were being built, but it didn't get done.

The forest devils attacked the settlement in broad daylight and Bert was killed. Everyone was scared out of their minds. Four men and two women were killed and several injured in that initial confrontation.

One of the beasts was killed. It wasn't a good showing for the settlers.

There were no warnings from anyone about the beasts. A Spanish detachment of soldiers stopped by once a month to check on the settlers. They gave no warning.

Some friendly natives had also begun to stop by on a regular basis to trade with the new whites. They gave no warning.

And a nearby trading post, run by two Frenchmen, had supplied the newcomers with supplies and even friendly advice about cabin construction, the upcoming winter and prime fishing spots on the river, among other things. They gave no warning.

Bert was one of the four men who were killed. A hasty meeting was held at the town square. It was chaos. The shouting and talking over each other was maddening.

Finally, Grammy couldn't take it anymore. She grabbed a loaded rifle from one of the men and fired it into the air.

She climbed up on a barrel of nails and spoke. She had learned to talk in a fashion that hid her education. Even though she had become the de facto doctor of the community, no one knew the depth of her learning.

"Quit your damn yelling and screaming over top of each other! You need to pick a leader! The stockade needs to be built at the same time as the town itself. It's to keep us in and them things out! We need us a shitload of firewood chopped so we don't freeze to death when winter comes. And ladies, you need to start putting up food stuffs and making jerky so we don't starve to death. And we need vegetables grown.

You can get your kids to help. They gotta chip in, if they're gonna eat. Now pick a man to oversee all that and do it fast, 'cause winter is three short months away!"

She got down to see what would transpire. She, honestly, could not think of one man that could lead this uneducated and raucous bunch of boneheads. She was beginning to wish she had never had come.

One man yelled, "I vote for Grammy to lead us!"

It was like watching children making dominoes fall. One person after another and then whole groups began shouting her name.

She climbed back up on that barrel of nails and held up her arms. Everyone got quiet. She actually liked the idea of being in charge. At least then she wouldn't have to live with mistakes made by idiots, no matter how well intentioned they might be. She knew she had seen enough other settlements and what worked and what didn't. She just couldn't seem too eager.

"You people really want a woman in charge? 'Cause I ain't gonna put up with none of you men second guessing my every move. You better rethink it."

"NO! You know what we need! Grammy for wagon master!" somebody yelled. And this was her point to herself. The time for a wagon master was over for at least three months now.

"Grammy for settlement leader!" someone else yelled. A few more titles were screamed from the crowd, but none quite fit her. She preferred not having a title.

Before the meeting broke up, she was in charge and countless people pledged their loyalty and support. The last thing she did was to tell the people to meet the next morning in the same place at sunup. She would have a plan by then.

And the next morning she did. She sent tree cutters into the nearby forest to fell trees for building and for firewood. She sent armed guards with them in case the unusual beasts returned.

She assigned men to start using half of those felled trees to build a stockade around their community. She determined which men were the most experienced homebuilders and that is what they did.

She had a group of women take over full time cooking chores for the settlement. She chose another group of women to grow vegetables, herbs and whichever fruits they were able. Another group took care of childcare for the youngest children in the community.

The older children were given multiple chores that supplemented the hands of the adults.

She also had a group of men build a hasty lookout tower that could see in all four directions. She didn't want to be surprised by natives, monsters, Spanish or even the occasional group of French trappers that passed through the area.

More important work was completed on that first day than in the previous two weeks. These people just needed direction. And she was just the woman to give it to them.

And now she stood in a cemetery with the Major of a United States Army unit. And she was grateful. The forest devils were becoming more aggressive, and it was getting cold. They weren't nearly ready for winter. The beasts had disrupted their well-planned schedule.

Unfortunately, she knew more had to die to make things better, and many deaths would occur in the Major's unit.

Chapter 5

Thornside

Grammy had whipped the people into shape. Her leadership skills helped the community to thrive. After she took over, the stockade moved along at a decent pace, but still wasn't finished, because they kept making the village larger.

At the point where Major Smythe entered the town, the stockade still had sixty feet to be fenced off. And that is where they had set their trap for the forest devils. The beasts continued to attack any area that was exposed.

The layout of the village was typical. There was a town square bound by the meeting house, the church, gaol and post office/medical building. There was one building on each side of the square.

In the center of the town was a well that had been dug down to the water table. Fortunately for the town, an underground spring ran under the town from north to south which guaranteed clean, cool water in abundance. There was some concern as to what that would mean during times of heavy rains and melting snow in the springtime. Perhaps that would be a problem for the town.

A building was constructed near the well to be used as a tavern and boardinghouse. A proprietor had signed a contract with the wagon master.

Other small buildings for contracted tradesmen were also built. A cobbler, silversmith, blacksmith/farrier, gunsmith, wigmaker and an apothecary topped the list, and they were given consideration as buildings sprang up.

A trading post, just inside the gate, was also included in their plans and was erected. When word of the new trading post got out, the two Frenchmen at the trading post on the river were not at all happy.

An octagonal magazine was built to hold extra weapons as they were acquired. They had their own small cannon, which no one knew how to use. It had belonged to the original wagon train master, who had been a cannoneer during the revolution for independence. It was now the sole occupant of the magazine, along with varying types of ammunition.

As to how the town acquired its name, it was given tongue-in-cheek. Grammy knew that their existence in this territory was going to be a pain in the ass for all concerned. But that was too crude a reference. So she suggested Thornside, referring to a thorn in one's side.

Most people agreed to the name. It went over the heads of quite a few and Grammy felt no need to explain it to anyone. A vote was taken, and most people were willing to do almost anything Grammy Hillburn wanted.

Thornside. But it wasn't the town that was the trouble.

Very quickly, the two French trappers learned that having another nearby trading post actually had its advantages. The relationship that had initially been hostile was now rekindled. There were no problems.

The Spanish detachment was now characterized, by Grammy, as twenty-five free-loaders looking for a meal as they passed through. They had no intention of enforcing Spanish territorial rights unless forced to. That was Grammy's unflattering opinion. They didn't prove to be a challenge of any kind.

The Quapaw did not appear overly concerned with the town, except for some light trading, and that was friendly. The Indians had actually provided valuable advice where putting up food stuffs for the winter was concerned. No threat existed from the natives.

The problem that had arisen was from the indigenous animals that the Indians have called the ste-te sh'a ta-ka. The natives had very little problems with them.

The settlers, however, had been at war with the beasts starting the third week since their arrival. The Indians believed that it may have been the spot on which they had chosen to build their town that was sparking the conflict.

The natives felt the beasts were dangerous, but discovered that if they left the creatures alone, the monsters of the forest reciprocated. The pioneers felt that they had somehow committed an unknown offense.

Grammy had no clue as to what they had done to arouse the forest devils, and she had no intention of giving in to the animals. As winter drew closer, the devils killed settlers every chance they got.

They attacked woodcutters, hunting teams and fishermen. The vicious animals also ventured into town, through the unfinished stockade, and attacked the builders as they worked.

Their work and productivity had been halved because half of the men and women who were able to fire a weapon were used as guards for the work crews. Fifty-eight pioneers had been killed thus far, almost twenty-percent of the community.

Almost all the citizens had staked claims, but no one was settling on those claims. All the homesteaders remained in the town for protection. Until the beasts were destroyed or tamed in some manner, land would remain unsettled and undeveloped.

The people that had signed on to the wagon train moving west were mostly uneducated laborers that wished for a better life for themselves and their families. Strangely, or maybe fortunately, the families did not boast a large number of children.

The more educated members included an apothecary, a lawyer, who had assisted with the land grant applications, a printer, who had brought his own printing press, the silversmith, a teacher for the children, an accountant and the son-in-law of a wealthy easterner who had died in one of the animal attacks. His death was the reason for the Army's current presence at the town.

Most of the folk were simple, hardworking people. This move was their chance to break free from a mundane existence and become landowners.

Among the citizenry were farmers, coal miners in that fast-rising industry, laborers from the glassworks near Pittsburg (the H had not yet been added), dairymen, lumbermen, seamstresses, washer women and two prostitutes looking for a new start. The ranks were filled out with a few other eclectic laborers.

And Grammy was their doctor. She made them understand that she was not a surgeon, by any means. She gave them that warning to decrease their expectations, but she had removed musket balls as well as assisted in a C-section delivery. She was more than capable to handle their needs. Many other towns along the frontier areas in the Spanish territory had no medical care at all.

As a fledgling community, the town had a good deal of experience and skills to draw upon. Things would have been moving at a brisker pace and the town thriving had the forest devils not shown up.

Just prior to the Army arriving, Grammy had rearranged the work crews to maximize the effort to finish the stockade. That plan was put into action, and Grammy got the idea to dig the pit to try to capture a forest devil.

She was as surprised as anyone when the trap worked.

Chapter 6

The Bait

The Major found himself back at the pit that held the hideous beast. He was mesmerized by its red eyes. They weren't glowing, but the overall effect was both eerie and astonishing at the same time.

The forest devil appeared to be able to communicate its contempt and hatred through its gaze. He wished the thing could talk, so they could find out what the beasts wanted.

Grammy had told him of the relatively peaceful coexistence the Indians shared with the beasts. And she shared that the natives had suggested that the pioneers had offended the animals by their choice of location for the town.

Major Smythe agreed with the old woman that they were the superior species, and they weren't moving. If only they could discern the offense that had these forest monsters so agitated.

The pitted monster growled and jumped up, clawing at the sides of the hole. It was, obviously, still favoring its right leg.

Lieutenant Elliot returned along with twenty-two men. Eight of them were the ranger contingent traveling with the two companies. The rangers were the elite fighters. They had undergone more rigorous training and been taught more combat skills than the regular army soldiers.

These rangers had been taught by Prussian mercenaries, noted for their ruthlessness and their appearance. They filed their teeth to points, both top and bottom. They were terrifying to behold. Their American students were forbidden from doing so by the United States government.

They were as tough as any fighting men on this continent. The other soldiers steered clear of them as much as possible.

The regular Army's uniforms were blue, white and red. The rangers' uniforms were green. They were expert scouts and trackers, and the green uniform was excellent camouflage.

Smythe was glad to have them. They had proven valuable against the Indians that had harassed them as they made their way to the Spanish territory.

The Lieutenant allowed each man to take a turn gazing down at the captive forest devil. He wanted them to know what they were up against.

Major Smythe watched the process with some amusement. Some men were frightened, but tried not to show it. Others were fascinated by an animal that they did not know existed. The rangers appeared amused.

Major Smythe was sure the rangers were acting amused to solidify their tough guy reputation in front of the other men. He wasn't sure whether the others were convinced or not.

Lieutenant Elliot told him that they planned to take up positions at dusk and wait to see if there would be any activity from the forest devils.

The Major rode out to his waiting Army encampment while it was still light enough to see the way. He would check back in the morning.

The encampment was close enough to the town that if guns were fired, they would be heard. He would post double the guards that were normally employed around the encampment.

At sunset, the Army detachment took their places in doorways, behind logs, firewood piles, barrels and every other convenient place to hide a man with a musket.

Now the waiting would begin.

The bait could be heard snarling in the hole. The first sign of engagement was a rock barrage that lasted what seemed like ten minutes, but in fact was only four minutes.

During that time, everyone had drawn back into whatever spot they were located to avoid being hit. When the rock barrage stopped, there was total silence.

As the men listened, one of the rangers low-crawled to the hole where the bait was held. He peered over the edge. The beast was still there, but lie immobile. Its growls and grunts had ceased.

There were several large rocks strewn about its body. Something was wrong.

The ranger called to his buddies, "Need light over here!" In a short period of time, another ranger emerged with a torch. He held the light for maximum advantage to illuminate the hole.

"It's dead! They stoned their own mate to death," one ranger announced.

The ranger with the torch inspected the ground around the hole. Large footprints that had not been there previously were now present.

The Lieutenant came out to the two rangers while the others stayed in place, just in case this should be a ploy by their new enemy.

Elliot asked, "What does this mean?"

"It means that the sons of bitches are smart. They kept us nailed up tight while a few of them rushed in here and killed our bait. For what reason, I don't know. But that is what just happened," Ranger Sergeant Camden reported.

"And they just left, instead of staying to fight?" Elliot asked.

And then they heard the gunshots from the encampment. The forest devils failed to engage the men who were ready to fight them, and instead, they conducted a sneak attack on the Army camp.

The sentries were alert for just such an incident to occur. Major Smythe had warned them.

The two guards fired their weapons at one of the beasts, and it howled in agony. But a second beast had circled behind them, grabbed them and crushed their skulls against two different trees.

Men with guns were scrambling everywhere.

Seven of the beasts entered the eastern edge of the camp where the women were billeted. Several women exited their tents in a panic. That was a mistake.

The devils pounced, killing them as quickly as they showed themselves. But before the beasts could enter the tents, a squad of men ran to their rescue, firing upon the hairy giants. More howls of pain could be heard.

Even more soldiers found themselves at the eastern end of camp. A few more gunshots later, two of the monsters lay dead. It was a costly incursion against a heavily armed enemy.

As the few injured were treated, the dead were gathered in one area. No one would sleep anymore this night.

The Major walked the entire perimeter and made sure a solid defense had been set. First Sergeant Lattimore accompanied him.

"If the beasts attacked here, it means they most likely knew we were ready for them in town," Smythe reasoned aloud.

"Jesus, Joseph and Mary, sir! You're talking like these animals got brains like men. You don't mean that, do you?" the First Sergeant asked.

"No, Lattimore. Just seems strange that they should be so lucky," the Major answered.

"Well, we killed two of the devils. I couldn't believe how big they are! And stink, sir! A skunk smells better than that," Lattimore, added the top enlisted man, added.

Lattimore was First Sergeant for both companies and had been under Smythe's command for almost seven years, harkening back to when he fought Indians in the Ohio Valley.

The First Sergeant was one of the men that Smythe had saved in the Battle of Fallen Timbers in 1794, while he himself was wounded. Lattimore would never forget this fact, and his gratitude made him a great pick to be Smythe's top enlisted soldier.

Lattimore's loyalty knew no bounds. Smythe always treated the man with respect and always made sure that the enlisted men knew that the First Sergeant had his ear. If you messed with or disrespected Lattimore, you were doing the same to the Major.

When morning broke upon the encampment, the sight of the dead forest devils in the daylight made a man's thoughts quickly turn sober. The women were the most frightened. Four of their friends had been killed.

The Major and Lattimore headed into town to check on Elliott and the rangers.

Upon their arrival, they immediately recognized Grammy Hillburn who was walking around to check on the same situation. Smythe was afraid of what they would find out. The only rifle play was from their own encampment. He was concerned by what that might mean.

The Major dismounted and approached Elliott at the same time that Grammy arrived.

"Your report, Lieutenant!" Smythe demanded.

"They killed the bait, sir."

Smythe was momentarily stymied.

"What in hell do you mean, they killed the bait?" Grammy asked, getting to the immediate and confusing point.

"They stoned it to death. Big rocks, too," Elliot said to Grammy. He then realized that he should be speaking to Smythe. "Sorry, sir. They stoned the injured the creature in the pit."

Grammy winced at Smythe, as if to say, what the hell were your pretty boys doing.

Smythe couldn't help but show that he was perturbed, "And what were you and your men doing, Elliot? Playing cards? Polishing your boots? How in God's good name could they come in and kill the bait? And your detachment didn't fire a single shot?"

"They used cover fire, sir," Ranger Sergeant Camden spoke up.

"Explain!" Smythe sternly said to the ranger.

"It is when you use a short, brief flurry of fire to cover men you are sending in to get closer to a target," the soldier in green said, defining the term.

"Are you saying they fired at you? With guns?" Lattimore chimed into the conversation and then looked at Smythe. "Excuse me, sir. That slipped out."

"Excused, Sergeant. It was my thought exactly," the Major admitted.

Camden opened his mouth, but Elliott answered, "They kept us pinned down with a barrage of rocks, and while we sought the safety of our surroundings, they rushed in and finished off their wounded comrade. It is a poor excuse, sir, but it is what appears to have happened."

Grammy was watching the proceedings with an amused look on her face.

The Major noticed and turned to her, "Question?"

"Yep. How many of the forest devils would it take to throw rocks at twenty-two armed men and keep them frozen in place? And how long did that barrage last, Lieutenant?"

Smythe nodded toward Elliott that he may answer her directly.

"The barrage lasted about five minutes, though it seemed longer. And the amount of good-size fodder that flew would have taken more than a dozen of the creatures, maybe two."

"That scares me more than anything. Their numbers may be more than we thought," Grammy admitted, and then she turned to Smythe. "Heard gunshots from your camp. What happened?"

"About ten entered our camp. We killed two, and from the sounds of them, we wounded a few others. Our casualty count was four soldiers, with two soldiers injured and four women laundresses killed. I think they were just testing us," he told her.

He continued, "Grammy, I want to move my encampment within the stockade. It will be terribly crowded, but we will help you, not only to finish building your stockade, but expand it a bit to accommodate us. You will end up with a larger fortified town. Is that okay?"

"Yep. Sooner the better. Get that damn wall done! And then maybe we can actually sleep at night," she responded.

"You heard her, Elliott. Take Sergeant Lattimore and tear down the encampment and bring it in here. In the meantime, Ranger Sergeant Camden and his men are going to explore beyond the wall and the pit with me and see if we can get a handle on how many beasts attacked us last night."

Camden immediately whistled twice. The other seven rangers came running and stood in a line, at attention.

Smythe almost laughed at how seriously they took themselves, but he controlled himself. And the thought that passed through his mind was that their serious attitude may be someone's saving grace one day. Maybe his own.

Chapter 7

Build that Wall

The Major and the rangers found several disturbing items in the field from which the forest devils launched their attack. That side of the settlement faced an open field before the tree line began.

It was mostly filled with weeds and thistles. What the rangers found as they explored was that a good portion of the field had been trampled flat. It was impossible to tell how many of the beasts had come into the walled town, but it appeared it was definitely more than ten, maybe twice that number.

The Major walked between the piles of rocks, five piles to be exact. The rocks were river rocks and were not from this field or the nearby forest. This meant that they chose their ammunition and brought it with them. They distributed that ammo into piles at optimum spacing to be launched in the most effective manner.

Smythe became more concerned than he had been. It was one thing if the monsters were simply opportunists and used what was immediately available, but this suggested something much more frightening. These animals were capable of planning and the execution of that plan.

Ranger Sergeant Camden knew what Smythe was thinking, "They are almost human, sir. These are not dumb animals. But knowing that will now help us eliminate them. We need to treat them like any other enemy."

The Major knew he was right. Maybe this was going to make things easier. The devils were not dumb animals and unpredictable. He could now plan to outsmart them.

The priority now had to become finishing the wall.

"Should we head into the woods, sir? Should we find more evidence of their attack?" Camden asked.

"No, Ranger Sergeant Camden. If they are almost human, that means they live in community. You and the rangers need to find where they live. That way, we can attack them."

"Yessir." Camden then whistled twice. The rangers came running and stood in a line, at attention, once again.

Smythe went from amused by this routine to impressed by it. He wished his entire Army would respond this well. He watched as the rangers faded into the woods.

After meeting with the Major, Grammy began her day looking at a young pregnant woman. The patient was over seven months along. Her husband sat outside, because Grammy had to put him out. His nervousness was transferring to his wife.

She was experiencing unexplainable cramping. Grammy determined that it was not due to the pregnancy. It was more likely something she had eaten. The young woman felt that way as well, but her husband insisted she be examined.

Grammy would normally find this amusing, but there were too many irons in the fire today. The Army moving in and the wall needing to be finished were at the top of the list. She was also scheduled to meet with the ladies who had been working at putting up various food stuffs for winter.

Grammy noticed that today was particularly cold and gray. The feeling of snow was in the air. Grammy had a sensitivity for those type of things. She would tell some people that she could smell it or feel it in her joints.

Two other patients showed up unexpectedly. They had minor complaints. Grammy took care of them and sent one to the apothecary.

By the time she stepped outside again, it was flurrying.

That wasn't bad news. The settlement had been expecting winter to set in any day.

When she checked on the wall progress, it was going slower than what she had hoped. But it was getting done, so that wasn't bad news.

The bad news was currently riding in through the front gate. Capitan Dominguez rode in with his cavalry detachment. They stopped and stared at the townspeople who were working alongside the heretofore unknown American troops.

Dominguez saw Grammy supervising the construction on the northern wall. He rode quickly to her side and dismounted.

"Senora Grammy, these are American soldiers helping you build your stockade. They are within the stockade, which means they are building a fortification, which is against the terms of your settlement. You are forbidden from building a military fortification."

"They are here to protect us against our enemies. Not the Spanish, of course," she quickly explained.

Major Smythe saw the man and walked over and introduced himself. The capitan saluted and Smythe returned the military greeting.

"Senor, what you are doing is expressly forbidden by my government. You cannot build a fort in Spanish territory. You should know this. And the Indians in these parts are not hurting the settlers. You are not needed here," Dominguez stated emphatically.

"Captain, we are not here to protect them against the natives. We are here to protect them from the forest devils," Smythe explained. He thought that made perfect sense.

Dominguez looked as if his command of the English language had disappeared.

"What is this forest devil?" the capitan asked.

"Hey! STOP!" Lattimore yelled. He was looking at three of the Spanish cavalrymen who had exited through the wall and were headed outside of the settlement.

Several of the American soldiers reached for their weapons. Things were getting tense quickly.

Smythe ordered his men to stand down. The three cavalrymen had pulled up and were waiting for Dominguez to give them an order.

"What are your men doing, Captain?" the Major asked.

"We are here to take the proper measurements for the placement of the settlement onto our maps. Surveying measurements," the Spanish officer explained. "But, of course, if you're building a fort, that is a moot point, because the fort must be destroyed and the occupants expelled."

"This is not a fort! And my troops were moved inside because we were attacked by the forest devils."

Again, Dominguez made a face, "What are these forest devils to which you refer?"

Grammy pulled Smythe aside, "He may not know about the creatures. He and his detachment are always passing through. They never stick around. Show them the two dead ones from last night and the one in the pit. Then he'll understand."

"Captain, walk with me," Smythe requested.

Dominguez followed the American officer to the edge of a large hole.

Smythe pointed, "That is a forest devil. They have killed fifty-eight of these people since they arrived."

The Captain's eyes were huge as he took in a species that he never knew existed, except as an Indian legend.

Dominguez turned to Grammy, "Why did you never tell us? We would have helped you."

"It was our fight, Capitan. And, no offense, but we really didn't want you around and getting underfoot," she admitted.

Dominguez turned to the Major, "And your soldiers were attacked?"

"Yes. So we just moved our encampment this morning. Eight people were killed last night. It seemed prudent to do so," the American officer explained.

"But, Senor, you are American soldiers in Spanish territory. Some would call this an act of war."

"No. We are only here to fight those animals. When they are eliminated, we leave. We mean no harm. Please don't take it any other way. This is not a fort!" Smythe again pleaded.

Smythe remembered his orders to avoid Spanish and French troops, if at all possible. It wasn't possible, since Grammy had told him that this Spanish cavalry unit stopped by every three to four weeks. He wondered how this was going to play out and how many more Spanish troops were in the area.

Dominguez realized his three surveying horse soldiers were still waiting for instruction, "Seguir!" he yelled.

The men responded immediately. Two dismounted and set up a tripod mounted theodolite. The other rider headed to the forest's edge to employ a stick with a graduated scale marked upon it.

All eyes were on the riders, out of curiosity. When the cavalryman with the stick reached the edge of the forest, everyone gasped.

Four forest devils emerged and attacked the horse and rider. The horse tried to rear up in fear, but the beasts overwhelmed the equine and took it to the ground, rider and all.

"Elliot!" Smythe yelled.

The Lieutenant barked orders and men grabbed their rifles and began running across the field.

Dominguez mounted his horse and led the cavalry out through the hole in the stockade and across the field.

The others watched in horror as one of the huge beasts bashed the horse's skull with a large rock. Two of the other devils broke a leg or two of the horse. And the fourth monster was rending an arm from the soldier.

Everyone saw it and gasped as the beast held the arm aloft, over its head in apparent triumph.

Before the American or Spanish soldiers could reach the scene, the giant forest monsters fled into the woods and were gone.

Once arriving at the point of the attack, the Spanish horse soldier was found to be alive, but bleeding out and going into shock. There was nothing they could do to save him.

The horse was dead. The bashing it had endured was enough to end its life. It had suffered two broken forelegs, which prevented it from rising. The forest devils had been efficient in their assault.

The Major had mounted his horse and traveled to the ambush sight, along with the Spanish cavalry. He looked at the scene and wondered why the animals would attack the lone victim, while so many looked on.

Were the forest devils sending a warning? Were they smart enough to realize how demoralizing this would be? Or was it happenstance? Maybe the rider got too close and they simply capitalized on the circumstances?

He turned to Dominguez, "I am sorry, Captain. Truly. Whatever you need from us will be provided."

"We will need to stay the night. I wish to learn more about these bosque diablos. I think some things have become clearer to me."

"How is that, Captain Dominguez?" Smythe asked.

"I currently ride with twenty-five men under my command. There used to be thirty-two. I sent four men out on patrol in this area, maybe one year ago. They never returned. The Indians claimed they knew nothing of my men, and I believed them. Our relations with the indigenous people were good. I assumed the men deserted."

"Go on, Captain," Smythe gently prodded.

"Six months ago, before Grammy and her people arrived, I sent three more men to this area. They too did not return. It made no sense. I was suspicious of the Quapaw, but that did not feel right. I stopped sending small patrols."

"And now you believe that the forest devils had something to do with it?" the Major queried, already knowing the answer.

"Yes, Major. I have seen it with my own eyes. We will help you kill them. We must," Dominguez promised.

It was the alliance that Smythe needed. The common goal of ridding the area of the horrible beasts would ensure that his Army could stay without incident.

Chapter 8

Finished

The day after the attack, the wall was being worked on at a fever pitch. The final log crew was sent out with twenty men for cutting and as many as guards. Five cavalrymen also joined the entourage that was guarding the lumbermen.

Oxen teams were used to haul each picket back to its intended position in the palisade. The work went on unhindered.

Grammy was glad to fill Dominguez in on what she knew about the forest devils, or diablos, as he called them. Smythe was learning more as well.

Dominguez came to the same conclusion as Smythe had, "So, from what you are telling me, our mutual enemy are not dumb animals but intelligent beings. And that, of course, makes them even more dangerous," the capitan concluded.

"Yep. Sons of bitches are smart as shit! Now, how do we draw them into a fight on our terms? Our bait idea didn't work. Still can't figure why they killed their own," Grammy stated, confused by their actions.

"I don't have an answer for that, unless it was a mercy killing. They'd rather be dead than captured. Which implies empathy for their own kind," Smythe concluded.

"I don't know anything about that, but watching them kill my man and his steed has convinced me they've done it before. Taking down a horse and rider is what I mean."

"Yes, Captain. They seemed pretty darn proficient at the process. The teamwork between them was amazing to watch. I agree. This wasn't their first time," the Major concurred.

"Okay. So they had done it before. How do we kill them all before they kill us?" Grammy asked in her usual no nonsense fashion. But she was noticing that she was employing more complete sentences and was a little less sloppy with her speech. Having these two educated men to converse with regularly was a treat.

"Why don't they bother the Indians?" Dominguez pondered aloud.

"The Indians told us that they steer clear of the beasts, and the beasts don't bother them. The only problem with that explanation is that we try to avoid them, and they come looking for us. I think that's a little weird, don't you?" she asked the two men.

"They don't bother the Frenchmen at the trading post either," Grammy continued. "Just us. Are we on some kind of burial ground that belongs to them? Or a sacred space? There was absolutely nothin' here when we arrived. And in our first three weeks here, we didn't see hide nor hair of them."

Dominguez tried to keep up with the American colloquialisms. He figured them out as he went. Hide nor hair was a new one for him, but he worked it out and found it amusing.

"Is it possible," Smythe began, "that once you started killing animals for food and felling trees, and that the beasts saw you as competitors for the available resources? Which seem plentiful to my accounting. Maybe it took three weeks for the forest devils to determine that you were staying and competing for the available food?"

"Well, shit! We're just guessing and that ain't getting us anywhere. We need to bring them out where we can shoot them. Maybe them cannons can help?" she suggested.

"Cannons, Senor? I thought this wasn't a fort?"

"Captain, a unit our size always travels with cannons. And this isn't a fort. If you insist, you can take the cannons and hide them if you wish. I can't see a scenario where employing them against the animals would be effective."

"If'n we can draw them out, don't you have what they call grapeshot?" the settlement leader asked.

"Yes, Grammy. But drawing them out is the stumbling block. And Captain, we got three of them That's all."

"Four," Grammy corrected.

"Where is there a fourth?" Smythe asked.

"In the magazine. It's the only damn thing in there. It was the play thing of Charlie Danby. He was our original wagon master. Got killed by Lenape Indians on the way out. We didn't know what to do with the damn thing. Ain't got anybody that can fire it.

"And that's how I knew about grapeshot. Charlie would go on about all the things that could come out the end of one of those damn things. All designed to kill and destroy."

Smythe looked at Dominguez, "Okay, four. Take all four if it makes you feel safer."

The capitan smiled, "No need. You are a man of honor. No one else I know would offer up their cannons if they planned to use them. You are a good man, Major. We are allies now. I wouldn't insult you by taking your cannons. And Senora Grammy is correct. Maybe grapeshot could be used against them. Who knows?"

Right then, there was yelling outside. The three of them hurried out to see what was happening.

What they saw was the community assembled at the northern wall, along with most of the soldiers. The hole in the stockade was two pickets thick and those last pickets were being pulled across the field by oxen teams.

The oxen drivers had made it into a race between the two animals. The dumb beasts were totally unaware that they were being pitted against one another. They were just straining at their loads the best they could.

Smythe saw the drivers as they got closer. One was an American soldier and the other driver was a Spanish cavalryman.

Draped across one oxen team's back was the flag of the United States of America with fifteen stars and fifteen stripes. The other oxen team sported the red and yellow Spanish War ensign bearing the off-center coat of arms.

Smythe, Dominguez and Grammy stood outside of the stockade with the others. Considering the events of the previous day, this competitive race was sorely needed to lift the spirits of the almost five hundred persons assembled on this spot in the Territory of Louisiana.

As the teams neared the make-shift finish line, the screaming increased. The lumbermen and their guards were trotting along behind the two oxen teams.

Smythe took in the smiles of his men and the people who were cheering. He hadn't realized it before, but smiles had been absent since they had arrived a few days ago. And now, for at least a short time, on this gray winter's day, there was joy and the feeling of real community and esprit décor.

A citizen of Thornside waved the white flag as the winning oxen team crossed the finish line. The Spaniards had won. It didn't really matter. Everyone was happy.

And no one was happier than Capitan Dominguez. He smiled at Smythe, "I wished we would have known about this a little earlier, Major. We could have placed a friendly bet."

"No. I wouldn't have wanted my men to refrain from being good hosts. Enjoy your victory," Smythe said, smiling from ear to ear.

Dominguez laughed and said, "Are you suggesting that your man let my man win?"

Now Grammy was laughing, "I believe that is exactly what he is suggesting, Capitan Dominguez. You could shut him up by taking his damn cannons."

The two men looked at each other, then they looked at Grammy and then they really shared a good laugh.

Chapter 9

The Rangers Return

An ox was slaughtered and roasted as the community celebrated the completion of the stockade wall. A few lookout towers still needed to be constructed, along with some ramparts and walkways, but the community was now enclosed and gated. It felt safe for the first time since the forest devils had shown themselves.

This would be the second night that the rangers were out. It wasn't that unusual. When the enemy was human, the rangers could use their skills to go undetected and avoid contact for days. Forest devils might be a completely different scenario.

Smythe was worried and Elliott and Lattimore were picking up on their commander's anxiety.

"Do you want me to take a detachment and look for them in the morning?" Lattimore asked.

"No. We have no clue which direction they may have gone. I just told them to find out where the beasts live. I hope I didn't hand them a death sentence," Smythe shared.

"Sir, them boys are too nasty to die. If they encounter those big animals, I think I'd feel sorry for the beasts," Elliot said, trying to lighten the mood.

"They'll be back soon, Major," Lattimore assured. "They know that staying out more than forty-eight hours doesn't do us any good, because we need information. I'd put my money on seeing them tomorrow."

"Let's hope. I'm going to check the walls. You two keep an eye on the men. And tomorrow, move our munitions into the magazine."

"Yessir," the two subordinates responded in unison.

Smythe walked away. Lattimore gave hand signals to two men who were standing on the edge of the festivities.

They understood that they were to escort the Major, just in case.

After walking about twenty yards, Smythe turned around, "Did Lattimore send you to be my guardian angels?"

"Yessir," one of them responded.

"Fine," Smythe sighed. He would have preferred to walk alone, but understood it was a sound practice to have an armed escort.

They walked the perimeter of the stockade. The Major noted where steps and walkways should be added. And a rampart could be needed if they ever had to employ a cannon from inside the stockade.

His mind wandered away as he walked with the two men. He began wondering what the rangers might have found. Did the things have a community, of sorts, deep within the forest? And the question he had from the very beginning was how many of them are there?

And then the question of their origin crept into his thinking. They walked upright, like humans. They were intelligent, beyond the realm of the animal kingdom that he was accustomed.

As a good Anglican, he had never questioned man's superiority and separateness from nature. To his knowledge, no one had. But here they were, faced with a beast that mimicked man on many levels.

They planned their attacks. They prepared and then carried the attack out with precision. First to kill the beast in the hole and then to drag down the Spaniard and his horse.

Even a pack of wolves, working together, were just opportunists. But the forest devils had an agenda. And they used rocks as weapons. He wondered if they used tools of any type. Would they find them using clubs or sharp sticks as weapons? Of course, with their great size and strength, it seemed unnecessary. The rocks made sense because they were a distance weapon.

He completed his tour of the settlement and dismissed his escort. He rejoined the celebration.

Grammy found him, "Why do you look so serious, Major? Finishing that wall was a great accomplishment to keep everyone safe."

"I know, Grammy, but I still have some men out there. I'm worried about them."

"Yes, the green men. That doesn't sound very soldierly. I mean, aren't you fellows tough as nails? Since when does a commander care so much about his men?" she asked.

"I'm not the only one. Good commanders realize that their men are their only assets in accomplishing the mission. If you mistreat them or disregard them, it will affect your ability to be successful," he explained.

"Mmm. Sounds like how I feel about my people. I don't want to lose anymore of 'em. Sometimes I wish I had been in charge from the beginning. I would have done some things different. But that is water gone under the bridge, as they say. Just gotta move forward and keep 'em safe. You helped with that. Thank you," she said in a moment of extreme sincerity.

"You're most welcome, Grammy. I'll set my men as guards tonight. Your people can get a good night's rest for a change."

The conversation ended, and shortly thereafter, the celebration did likewise. It would have lasted longer had there been more libations. The tavern owner was working on a few batches of beer, but they weren't yet ready.

The settlement got quiet. The guards were set. The community slept soundly. The soldiers were relieved as well. The Spaniards had joined in the revelry, and now they too took turns keeping watch during the night.

Smythe retired to his tent to find Constance waiting. She had the small stove stoked, and the tent was warmed for his arrival.

She began talking about the baby the women were taking care of. She wouldn't cease. It was maddening.

"Stop, Constance! I am weary, and I'm not up for conversation, nor carnal pleasures. Please retire so that I may get some rest."

"So, I am dismissed, like one of your foot soldiers? You don't want to be sexed up, so leave. Is that it?"

"That is the way its always been. I am married. You know that," he reminded her.

"Yes. Married for over two years to a woman with who you have had sex with once, and that wasn't even consensual. You and I, however, have engaged in the act many times. Over one hundred times at least. I am more your wife than she is."

"What is your point?" he asked.

"I have been saving myself for you. You know, the other men want me, but stay away because I am the Major's whore. If you aren't going to lay with me, I might as well make money with the others."

"Then I release you. Make a living like the others. I shouldn't have brought you out here. It was a mistake."

She stormed out of his tent without another word spoken. He was too exhausted to care. The Major quickly settled into a rhythmic breathing as rest overtook him.

Morning arrived soon enough.

Smythe was a light sleeper. He heard the call that the rangers were approaching. This was the practice when the gates were closed, to announce approaching persons. Opening the gates was beyond the paygrade of the guards. They needed an order to do so.

Smythe quickly put his boots on and assembled his uniform. His rule was to never look sloppy in front of his men. Elliot was the same way. He wished Lattimore was a little less slovenly, but that was overlooked for all his other good qualities. One of them would have to give the order to open up for the approaching contingent.

The Major left his tent and headed to the gate. He was met on the way by Grammy Hillburn.

"It's your green men, ain't it?" she asked.

"Yes, Grammy. They have returned."

"I know they'll have a lot to tell you. I'd like to sit in on that meeting, if you don't mind?" she requested.

Had this been a time of war, the answer would have been no. But this was different, and he felt she had a right to know what was going on, if they had anything great to tell.

Smythe ordered, "Open the gate! Guard the breech!"

As the gate opened, Lattimore ordered about ten men to standby. If anyone or anything tried following the men into the stockade, it would be met with resistance.

It was obvious that nothing was following them, and the tree line was far enough away that no surprise could be enacted, but it was military protocol. It was a good practice to maintain.

Ranger Sergeant Camden stepped forward.

"Sergeant Camden, reporting in, sir. We have much to discuss with you, but I and my men are starving. May we partake of nourishment before we meet?"

"Absolutely, Sergeant Camden. I believe you will find leftover oxen in the mess tent. Report to me after you eat and clean up a bit. And dismiss your men after they have eaten. We'll talk in the meeting house."

"Yessir," the Ranger Sergeant responded.

"Grammy, let's give them some time. We'll go to the meeting house in about thirty minutes."

Smythe informed Elliot and Lattimore of the plan.

The Major was eager to hear what they had discovered, as were they all. Hopefully, it would be something that could bring this mission to a conclusion.

He walked over to the area where the Spaniards were staying and invited Capitan Dominguez to join them. The cavalry leader was grateful for the invitation.

Chapter 10

What They Found

"We followed the trail that the beasts had left after they had attacked the settlement and killed the creature that was used as bait. The area that was trampled, initially, told the story of at least a dozen creatures being involved. And at least one human," Camden stated.

"Initially?" Grammy questioned.

Camden looked at Smythe, unsure of protocol since the old woman had asked the question. Smythe nodded his consent to answer her directly.

"Well, ma'am, they appear to be smart. Shortly after we started to follow the trail, it split into three separate trails. It is like they knew to split up to increase the difficulty of being followed. That's not normal animal behavior. And the human tracks had gone with one of the three groups."

"So what did you decide to do, Sergeant Camden?" the old woman asked. That is how Grammy was perceived, as the old woman. But, in fact, she was only fifty-four years old. She had begun to play the part of the wise, old sage, no longer fixing her hair or employing any adornments whatsoever. Her time in the Louisiana Territory had convinced her that men and love were unnecessary distractions.

"We decided to simply pick a trail and let it take us where it may. So I chose the one that included the human footprints. It went on for the longest time, and then met back up with another trail. A little while farther, it seemed as if the whole herd had reunited."

"Herd?" Capitan Dominguez questioned. "Why did you choose that term?"

Once again, Camden looked at his superior and received the unspoken permission to answer the Spaniard directly.

"Captain, I don't know why I used that term, other than the fact that it looked like a herd of cattle had moved through the forest. But it was where it came out that had us all confused." Camden stopped and looked nervously at Major Smythe.

It was Smythe's turn, "Now the plot thickens. So where did this herd of forest devils end up so that they confused you?"

"At the Quapaw Indian village. We all felt sure we were going to see signs of a massacre. But as we observed the village, nothing seemed out of place. Everything was what I would consider normal. Even tranquil. No sign of a forest devil raid. So, yessir, we were legitimately confused because the trail obviously ended right there."

"Did you get past your confusion, young man?" Grammy asked, hoping the answer would be yes.

"Yes, ma'am. We stayed in hiding and observed the Indian village. On the second day, our confusion was cleared up quickly. And we understood, at least in part, how a set of human tracks got mixed in."

Elliott and Lattimore looked on and never said a word. They sat, taking it all in. They were both pleased that their unit now knew the location of the Indian village. Or would know, after the rangers mapped it out for them.

Camden returned his attention to Smythe, "May I continue, sir?"

"Yes, Sergeant. And we will all hold our questions until you are finished," Smythe promised for all to hear.

"On the second day, we saw a forest devil walking through the camp. No one was paying him any attention. No one screamed or moved themselves away from the beast. He disappeared into one of their lodges. The lodge was taller and wider than all the others. And its shape was different. Most dwellings were the traditional pointed dwellings.

"A bit later, we saw three devils exit with an Indian that seemed to be giving them instructions. They walked out of the village together and walked up the rocks that are behind the native encampment. Strategically, the village is indefensible. An opposing force could pick them apart from the overlooking cliffs and rocks.

"But we continued to be patient. We saw a few more forest devils come and go. We needed to see the inside of that lodge. We waited for evening. I sent Tyrell and Walters in to check more closely as to why this dwelling was different, and why the forest devils came and went so freely through the door of that particular lodge." Camden paused and took a drink from his canteen.

"Good Lord, Sergeant! Did you attend theatre school? You have us all in suspense, now get to the damn payoff!" Grammy scolded.

Camden didn't appreciate her outburst. It made him look foolish, because he was drawing it out because he liked feeling important and being listened to. And the way he saw it, he was the only one in the room who had anything interesting to say.

Smythe was amused, but had to maintain order, "Miss Hillburn, you are here as a guest in a military meeting. Please control yourself, or I will ask you to leave."

Grammy was duly embarrassed by his warning.

Camden felt a great deal of satisfaction at the Major's reprimand of the old woman. It was short lived.

"Having said my piece to Miss Hillburn, I must agree with her in that we need information, and we need it now. Sergeant, be more forthcoming with what you observed."

Camden's ears burned. No one should talk to a ranger like that. The Major was now on what he called his 'shit list.'

As directed, he continued, "My men discovered that the strange lodge masked the entrance to a large cave opening that went downward into the earth. They estimated it went in a direction that put it under the village's western half. The beasts are, literally, living under the Indians.

"After that information was learned, we headed back here. That is my report, sir."

"Excellent job, Ranger Sergeant Camden. Once again, you and your men have proven to be invaluable," Smythe complimented him to smooth the man's ruffled feathers.

"Is there anything else you saw that would be important to us tactically or otherwise?" Smythe continued.

"They smell bad, sir. My men told me that it took everything they had to keep from vomiting. That may be helpful at some point."

"Thank you, Sergeant. You are dismissed. Good job."

"Thank you, sir." Camden left, glaring at Grammy.

"Your green man don't like me, Major. I guess I better watch my back," she said, not meaning to be humorous.

It was Capitan Dominguez that cut the tension when he advised, "Senora Grammy, if he offers you food or drink, I wouldn't take it."

Laughter filled the room.

The tense feelings returned quickly as they processed what the rangers, or as Grammy called them, the green men, had learned.

"Captain, have you ever been to the Indian village?" Smythe asked.

"Yes. Many times. The lodge of which he spoke, I have seen it many times. The Indians always come out to greet us. Everyone comes out, including men, women and children. They always move us along quickly. We have never really gotten very far into the village," Dominguez stated, thinking about it for the first time.

"You weren't suspicious, Captain?" Elliott asked.

"No. There was no reason. We are the strangers in their land. We are the occupiers. I just figured they didn't like us, and I could not blame them."

"How many Indians would you estimate are in the village?" Smythe asked Dominguez.

"Maybe two hundred in total. But warriors? Maybe only sixty or seventy," the Spaniard guessed.

Chapter 11

Moving Forward

One the first things that Smythe did, after the meeting broke up, was to find Ranger Sergeant Camden. He wanted the Sergeant's estimate as to the population of the village and the number of warriors. His numbers were very close to what Dominguez had estimated.

The natives, as a fighting force, could be easily overwhelmed. But if they attacked the village, would that bring the forest devils to the surface?

There was only one way to find out.

Capitan Dominguez explained to his men exactly what the rangers had observed. Each one was prepared to avenge the death of their fallen comrade in arms.

They were, however, surprised to hear about the Indians' involvement. Their immediate response was to start cleaning their weapons and sharpening their lances, daggers and swords.

Each cavalryman had a sword, a unit designated dagger, a pistol, a short-barreled musket and a lance. The cavalry unit was considered an elite fighting unit in the Spanish military complex and had been for hundreds of years.

Dominguez and his unit had come in through New Orleans, accompanying a Spanish diplomat. The diplomat had returned to Spain, but the cavalry unit was asked to stay behind and help tame the Louisiana Territory.

Dominguez and his men were not happy with how they were abandoned so far from home. Many of the men had families and sweethearts. The bottom line for the proud Spanish fighting men was duty and honor.

They carried out their assignment faithfully. The unit had now been stuck here in the failed Spanish colonial expansion for four years.

There was no doubt they had become somewhat lax in their duties. And the reason was simple. Their duties were never clearly defined. Dominguez was making up the rules as he went.

Given maps at the outset, they endeavored to see the entire northern territory. They added to the maps, where they were able. They noted American settlements and Indian villages.

It was actually the Americans that showed them proof of the land offers by Spain. That happened months before a Spanish official, who had been traveling with a few bodyguards and a group of monks, confirmed it for them. But their duties continued to remain undefined.

It was frustrating for the capitan. He was intelligent enough to know what type of expectations that would be put upon them. So he carried out a plan of his own making.

Mapping the settlement was going to be his excuse to get his men back to New Orleans and hopefully out of the country. He could only hope it would work, but first the Indians and forest devils must be dealt with.

Dominguez had fielded several attempts by Major Smythe to establish Spanish troop strength in the area. The Capitan had been purposefully vague every time. It was easy, because he wasn't sure.

As far as Dominguez knew, his current unit of twenty-four riders and himself were the only Spanish military presence in the entire northern part of the Louisiana Territory.

He then thought of the two patrols he had sent out and had never returned. Even though he couldn't believe they would desert, he had no other choice but to believe it to be true.

But now, he was afforded another explanation. One that made more sense, and it made his blood boil. Yes, the Indians would pay for their complicity with the monsters, and the monsters were going to be exterminated.

Grammy was meeting with Sergeant Lattimore. They were laying the groundwork for a militia. He was teaching her structure and the inner workings of an Army made up of citizen soldiers.

The impending attack on the Indian village made putting a civilian fighting force together an imperative. To ensure an overwhelming victory, a militia would need to back up the soldiers.

Although it was true that the people of Thornside had fought together several times before, that was only in defense of their settlement. Lattimore was trying to make Grammy understand that an attacking force was a different animal altogether. And that was how he put it, a different animal.

Grammy's only comment was, "Sergeant, we're starting to become experts on different animals."

Lattimore told Grammy she needed to choose a commissioned officer and four noncommissioned officers. In this case, a lieutenant and four sergeants.

She thought for several moments. She put her quill pen to a piece of linen paper and wrote some names for consideration. Grammy hated wasting writing paper, but this task was important, and she needed to record her thoughts.

The outcome achieved was that Morris Turner, the silversmith, would be asked to be the lieutenant. His sergeants would be the Bannister brothers, Matthew and Luke, Thomas Grissom and Peter Ellsworth.

Turner was older than the men nominated to be the noncommissioned officers. He had fought in the War for Independence, which most called the Revolution. He hadn't been an officer in the Continental Army, but he had led a group of minutemen for two years. Their guerilla tactics had helped to disrupt the British response.

The other four had been minutemen at one time or another during the Revolution, as they were needed. They were all good men, and Grammy had made thoughtful choices.

It was a good start. Grammy sent the Porter boy, who had just brought in some firewood, to find the men. An hour passed before all five men were in the room with Grammy and Lattimore. None of the men balked at the responsibility being offered to them.

Lattimore began a new set of lessons, ones that discussed the duties and skills of a soldier. The men listened intently, partially because they knew how important this new job was and partially because they wanted to please Grammy.

 She had truly won everyone's respect, except a few hard cases, and she had also earned their gratitude for getting them this far. Everything that these people did, on a daily basis, was for their personal survival and the continued health of the settlement.

Over the next several days, Sergeant Lattimore drilled sixty men, who would make up the militia. It was a tall order to whip them into a military mindset.

The two youngest militiamen were only sixteen years old. It was the minimum age that they agreed upon. Grammy was pushing for eighteen and Lattimore wanted it to be fifteen. He discovered that there were four boys, all fifteen years old, just ready and chomping at the bit to be soldiers. Grammy refused. She personally knew the boys, and she insisted they were mentally too young. They finally agreed on a minimum age of sixteen after much debate, which included the newly commissioned Lieutenant Turner.

They learned to march, volley fire, countermarch and to follow orders, in general. Speed loading their rifles was taught by the rangers.

Some of the men picked up the various lessons faster than others. It was evident that all the men were giving their best effort. Grammy was proud of them.

On their last day of training for the week, the men were broken down into squads. The breakdown of the company was simple. There were four squads of fifteen men each, headed by a sergeant. Lieutenant Turner was the company commander to which the sergeants reported.

To promote esprit de corps, it was decided that the men would wear a buckskin hunting shirt, which most of the men already owned. They would also wear buckskin breeches and a blue tri-corn hat. Several of the ladies in the village were working hard to make sure the men all had these three items of clothing.

The militia, sixty-five strong, will back-up the regular Army in battle. After the regular Army eventually leaves to return east, the militia will be the main protection for the settlement to guard against the natives and the forest devils, if any remained.

After drilling hard for days, the militia would have Sunday off. They were glad for the opportunity to rest. The weather was turning colder, and a day of warmth by the hearth appealed to most.

The regular Army spent their time patrolling the nearby woods to make sure they were not being observed and to not allow anyone, or anything, an opportunity to attack the settlement.

In addition, the regular Army was preparing its cannons and the former wagon master's cannon for service. Each man, like the Spaniards, were servicing their weapons.

Several groups of men had also been cutting firewood to stave off the increasing bitterness. Nighttime temperatures were falling into the twenties. Sleeping in the tents was becoming increasingly uncomfortable.

Several fires around the tents were kept stoked continually. Small stoves were also used. The cooks kept a constant supply of coffee and tea available to warm the men. There was talk of moving the soldiers into some of the larger buildings.

Hunting teams were having success and were bringing back deer, turkey and several wild boars. The area was rich in game. The Army and the members of the settlement were at least well fed, if not warm.

Eight inches of snow fell on Sunday night. The next morning, tracks were discovered in the snow, all around the stockade.

Chapter 12

Decisions

Smythe, Dominguez, Elliott, Lattimore and the rangers evaluated the prints. The consensus was simple. They weren't human. The footprints were far too large.

The rangers quickly followed the prints to the tree line and then returned. Ranger Sergeant Camden addressed the assembled men, "There's at least ten, maybe twelve."

"Why did they come, if only to walk around the settlement?" Dominguez asked.

"My guess is that they were looking for a weak spot in the wall. And to look closely at the wall," Smythe replied.

Ranger Sergeant Camden offered, "Claw marks can be seen about ten to eleven feet off the ground. The pickets are each only sixteen feet high. That's about an eight-foot creature with a three-foot reach. I wonder how high they can jump?"

"Maybe they are too heavy to jump very high. I am more inclined to think that they are so strong, that a dozen of them could ram the wall and knock it down, if they found a weak spot," Elliott added.

"Why didn't our guards see them? Or at least notice them in some way?" Elliott asked.

"Because we don't have walkways up yet. As much as we have built walls to keep things out, we are being boxed in. The priority today should be the walkways, so we can see over the wall," Smythe insisted.

"And the walls should be reinforced, in some way," Elliott insisted.

The group of men returned to the safety of the inner stockade. Ranger Sergeant Camden sent three of his men to follow the tracks back into the woods.

Dominguez pulled Smythe aside, "This is starting to look like a fort, Senor Major."

Smythe couldn't disagree with him. That was what a stockade essentially became when manned by soldiers. This was a fort.

"Captain Dominguez, it is starting to look that way. But I promise you, once the natives and the monsters are defeated, we will leave. We do not seek to steal land or push the Spanish out of this territory. My country has enough problems right now, recovering from the war. We just want our citizens to be safe."

"I've said it before, Major. You are a man of honor. I trust you. I count on you to not betray that trust," Dominguez stated, offering his hand.

Smythe shook it and prayed that they didn't receive orders from Washington to stay ensconced in the region. He wished to keep his word to this man.

As the day wore on, laborers began building walkways around the perimeter. The walkways would also help in reinforcing the walls.

An earthen rampart, at the northern and southern walls, would have to wait until spring. Currently, the ground was too hard for digging, and the American Army and Spanish cavalry were taking up too much space within the stockade.

Something eventful occurred later in the day. A five-man cavalry detachment came looking for Capitan Dominguez. He was as surprised as anyone.

They learned that the detachment had moved from settlement to settlement and homestead to homestead following his route. The Capitan's faithfulness to his duty, watching over the new American frontiersmen, had given them the trail that they needed to find him. It appeared that everyone knew of Dominguez and his men.

The detachment, led by Sergeant Emilio Garcia, had some news to impart. It was big news to Dominguez and his men, and it forced them to make an important decision.

"Capitan Dominguez, I have been asked to find and inform you that you, and your men, are being recalled to Spain. A grateful nation has appreciated your service in the Louisiana Territory, and you will be reassigned upon your return," Sergeant Garcia informed him.

Dominguez was surprised. His men whooped and hollered. This was good news indeed.

"May I ask, why now? We would have liked to return several years ago, so this is wonderful news. But the timing makes me curious."

Smythe, Elliott and Lattimore were present and were hearing the entire exchange. They were as curious as Dominguez.

Sergeant Garcia obliged the Capitan with an answer that stunned all who heard it, "Although France wishes this information to be kept secret, Spain no longer owns the Louisiana Territory. The French have purchased the land from his royal highness, Carlos IV. Our troops, governors and ambassadors are all be recalled."

Dominguez was not taking the news joyously, yet he had waited for this exact moment, like everyone else. His men took notice and ceased their revelry.

Dominguez's second in charge, Corporal Antonio Vargas, stepped forward, "Capitan Dominguez, with all due respect, you are not taking this as we expected. May we know why?"

"Our job here is unfinished. Seven of our brethren are missing and one was murdered in front of our eyes. We have been preparing to help our American friends set things right with the natives and the monsters. I cannot leave until that is done."

Sergeant Emilio Garcia asked, "What are these monsters of which you speak?"

Dominguez told him everything. His men stood there, shaking their heads in affirmation, and Smythe stepped forward and confirmed that it was all true.

"What do you wish us to do, Capitan?" Garcia asked.

Dominguez turned to his men and said, "For those of you who wish to leave now, do so with no hard feelings. I know many of you are married or have sweethearts waiting for you. Leave with Sergeant Garcia, and I will catch up with you later."

Smythe was shocked by what he witnessed. Not one of those remaining twenty-four men would leave their Captain. And to make it even more unbelievable, Garcia and his men refused to leave. Major Smythe could only hope to inspire this kind of loyalty from his men.

Dominguez was now the Captain of twenty-nine men, and his new second-in-charge was Sergeant Garcia. Having more cavalry during the attack would strategically be a definite plus.

Smythe, Dominguez, Elliott, Lattimore, Camden, Garcia and the new militia leader, Lieutenant Turner, met in the town meeting hall to strategize.

Grammy came and went, as several medical emergencies presented themselves, along with the builders of the walkways having questions. Smythe could not help but be impressed by her ability to handle so much. He had seen many men crack under much less stress.

About four inches of the original eight inches of fluffy snow had melted, leaving the rest as slush. This would become icy starting at sundown. For those fairly adept at reading the skies, tomorrow would be sunny like today and become warm enough for more melting.

Camden had already reported that once again his men had found human tracks amongst the monsters' tracks. He also raised a concern that the melting snow would make tracking difficult.

Dominguez told them that this was typical for November. Snow would come and melt away before the next winter storm dropped more.

He warned them that the really ugly weather could be anticipated in January through mid-February. Sometimes it could last until mid-March.

Dominguez turned to the ranger and said, "Ranger Sergeant Camden, you will get the chance to track in the snow soon enough."

They acknowledged that a large portion of the walkway was up on two walls. It should afford the night guard a fairly clear view of the open areas on all four sides of the settlement, until intruders would get closer to the walls.

With good weather predicted and defensive positions looking better around the stockade, they were able to plan for an assault. They now had massively superior numbers, plus the advantage of having both infantry and cavalry.

The disagreements came when Dominguez suggested their good fortune to have artillery as well. Smythe was reluctant to use it, except for defense of the settlement.

It was Ranger Sergeant Camden that turned the corner in the Major's thinking.

"Sir," Camden began, "we know which lodge hides the cave entrance. We also know the cave entrance faces east. Why not destroy the lodge with a few rounds of split shot, and then focus a bombardment on the cave opening as the creatures emerge? We could wipe half of them out before any real resistance is given."

All eyes were on Major Smythe. It was an excellent suggestion. In his mind, he reasoned that it would also cause massive chaos among the natives. The Army foot soldiers could sweep in and eliminate the natives, and the cavalry could run down any of the enemy that made it past the Army.

"Sergeant Camden, that is an excellent idea. Bombard first, sweep in with infantry and have the cavalry clean up the stragglers and escapees," Smythe explained to them.

A voice from behind them asked, "Men, women and children?" It was Grammy. She had returned from her many important duties.

"What do you suggest, Senora Grammy?" Dominguez asked.

They all listened respectfully. The question she asked would have had to have been addressed eventually.

"Well," she began, "if you kill all the men, but leave the women and children, they will eventually seek vengeance. They have already shown contempt for us whites, by harboring the forest devils. You have to kill them all, or we will be fighting this battle again and again. We have lost enough white lives to them sons of bitches. Fix the damn problem right the first time! That's all I got to say on the matter."

The old woman turned and left them to their discussion.

An hour later, the meeting broke up. Grammy saw Lattimore walking across the commons toward the Army encampment. He saw her and gave her a thumbs up. All the natives would be destroyed.

Chapter 13

The Natives

The Quapaw, also known as the Arkansa(s) Indians, had originally settled in the Ohio Valley region. They, and other tribes in that area, were driven west across the Mississippi by the Iroquois Indians, who were looking to expand and establish their hunting grounds.

The Iroquois regularly harassed the lesser tribes, but unexplainably backed off from any contact with the Quapaw. The Quapaw Nation migrated farther southwest towards the Oklahoma Territory.

The group that Grammy and Smythe were facing had remained behind. They were a small group that had lost favor with the larger Quapaw community.

There were rumors shared among the trappers, traders, French and Spanish settlers, as few as there were, and other native tribes. Grammy and Smythe had not heard the rumors. Capitan Dominguez had heard them, but dismissed them for he had not witnessed anything to support such a claim.

The rumor was that they practiced what Christians would describe as the black arts or even witchcraft. Whatever they believed was enough for them to be excommunicated by the larger Indian nation.

This band of Quapaw were led by a chieftain named Mi Soke, which means Sun Dog. He was an old man but greatly feared. When most chieftains reached their late fifties, they would be challenged by a younger man for the leadership of the tribe. Mi Soke was in his seventies, but no public challenge materialized.

Some said that Mi Soke had never been challenged. Others insisted that challengers simply disappeared once they made their intentions known. The old chief ruled his tribe with an iron hand, and his people feared him more than respected him.

He had five medicine men who did his bidding among the people. They, too, were feared. It wasn't that the members of the tribe were unhappy. They lived a relatively safe existence and were unmolested by other tribes, particularly the Iroquois.

The whites had been held at bay as well. Other natives disliked the encroachment of the Europeans and now the Americans. But this band of Quapaw had no concerns. They had the forest devils to protect them.

The Quapaw did not call them forest devils. That was what the whites had named them. The natives called them ste-te sh'a ta-ka, which meant, tall devil. The names were similar. Both peoples saw them as devils and not natural to this world.

The tall devils did not bother the Indians. It was believed, by the Quapaw, that Mi Soke alone had the power to keep them at bay.

He also controlled them in other ways, such as using them to attack their enemies. Most of the Quapaw knew they were walking a thin line between peace, safety and their own destruction.

Beyond the tall devils, village life was fairly mundane. They had prepared for winter, just as the whites had done. Their diets included jerky and dried fish for protein. Fruits and vegetables were either dried or preserved in brines in the many clay pots that were buried underground to be kept cold.

Daily hunting parties were sent out and supplied fresh game. Fishermen would sometimes have success, but the fish were going deeper in the nearby lake and ponds. Soon there would be no fish until spring.

The natives wore mostly animal skins and clothing made of blankets, bartered for at the trading post. Some European shirts and jackets could be seen being worn in the village as well.

The children of the village worked alongside the adults. Life was too hard to afford the luxury of play once a child reached seven or eight years old.

This band of Quapaw no longer believed in the Great Spirit. Mi Soke saw to that. They worshipped a dark spirit named Ta na De-ze, which meant Thunder Tongue.

Thunder Tongue required a sacrifice every spring. It was required that a virgin, at least thirteen years of age, be given to the tall devils to take underground.

This was all communicated to the tribe through Mi Soke. Most did not question the practice.

Mi Soke had been a great Algonquin warrior. His victories included those over other Indian tribes. He had fought alongside the French against the British.

During his time fighting alongside the Europeans, he learned their dishonorable ways and developed a hatred towards the whites. Mi Soke also lost faith in the Great Spirit, as he saw the whites stealing Indian land time and time again.

He began seeking another spirit to which to give his allegiance. Ironically, it was a European that introduced him to the dark arts and to the various names of the dark spirit. Satan, Lucifer or Beelzebub did nothing for him linguistically. He made up his own name for the devil, Thunder Tongue.

The idea for sacrificing virgins came to him from a Frenchman who had insisted it was a necessary practice. So it became part of his understanding and practice. As a younger man, he would rape the virgins before the sacrifice. As an old man, it was no longer an imperative.

As for the current practice, the people could only imagine what the giant beasts did with the maidens and how quickly their young lives were snuffed out. Parents of young girls lived in fear all winter long. Some fathers purposely deflowered their own daughters to save their lives.

The usual result was that Mi Soke would become incensed and kill the father, who had done the unthinkable. Several young maidens' lives were saved that way.

The tall devils walked around the village day and night, unhindered. They spent a good deal of their time foraging for food and game to sustain their large bodies. Wintertime was the most difficult.

The village currently housed seventeen tall devils. Sometimes the beasts would steal food from the villagers. Mi Soke would punish them, and on two occasions, he executed the culprits.

Now on this winter day, Mi Soke found himself in council with his medicine men. The tall devils were the topic of discussion. They had never had so many devils living amongst them before. Opportunities had presented themselves to grow the clutch of beasts and the Indians did so, knowing that they may need them some day.

But now it was winter. The huge creatures competed with the villagers for food. The herd needed to be thinned out.

Killing them off would be a waste. But sending them up against the enemy would be a perfect solution.

If the enemy, in this case the whites in the settlement, could be killed, demoralized and frightened, then that was a good thing. In the process, hopefully, several of the beasts would be killed. That would be a win/win outcome.

Mi Soke still thought the natives' secret was safe. He thought no one had made a connection between the redskins, which is what the whites sometimes called the natives, and the beasts.

He was wrong, but would it matter?

Chapter 14

The Attack

The next morning, the cannons were cleaned and readied for battle. They would march on the native village in the wee hours of the morning. They would be prepared for battle when the sun rose high enough to be able to see their enemies as they ran in disarray.

The cannons would destroy the lodge and then bombard the cave entrance as the monsters emerged.

The regular Army would sweep in from the west to begin their extermination plan as soon as the natives exited their teepees.

The Spanish cavalry would prevent anyone from escaping on the south side of the village. The north side was rocks and cliffs as Camden had described earlier.

And the militia would wait at the eastern end of the native encampment which would be the only exit route remaining.

The plan was set. They would leave the fort at 1:00 a.m. and head for the native village. The rangers had assured Smythe that they would reach the village after about marching for three hours.

At midnight, inside the settlement, soldiers began to stir as they lined up the cannons around the commons. The cannoneer teams were preparing the guns to be hooked up to caissons, which would then be hooked up to the horses that would pull them.

They prepared, not only the company's three cannons, but also the fourth, which had belonged to the deceased wagon master. The men inventoried three types of shot: Cannon balls, split shot and some grapeshot, if needed. That ammo was then loaded into the caissons.

The split shot was two halves of a cannonball held together by a chain. When shot, it would tear through the lodge, doing maximum damage to the structure.

The regular cannonballs would be used to fire at the opening of the cave. For those rounds that entered the mouth of the cave, they would travel down and hopefully kill a few forest devils, or at least strike fear into the beasts.

The grapeshot would only be used if the natives mounted a counter-attack and tried to rush the cannons. Grapeshot was the equivalent of a large, wide shotgun blast.

The cannoneers were excited to be pressed into service. They continued to prepare their equipment as other soldiers began to slowly muster at the town center.

The guards on the walkways were bundled up against a chilling wind. Unfortunately, those men assigned to be the lookouts, and the settlement's first line of defense, were paying more attention to the activity inside the fort than they were to the activity outside the fort.

They didn't believe it possible that on the same night that they were planning to attack the Indians and the forest devils that the beasts would attack them first. But it was about to happen.

The previous evening, the beasts had determined the weakest part of the stockade wall. It was the gate itself, and that is where they began their attack.

A group of forest devils and a medicine man snuck across the field on the southern corner. The nearest guard had his back to them the entire time.

Eight of the ten beasts present charged the gate and hit it with their shoulders. The gate buckled inward, and the entire stockade shook.

It was so sudden and unexpected that no one knew what had happened. That confusion gave the beasts another run at the weakening gate.

Their second hit cracked the heavy beam that held the gate shut. Another two or three charges at the gate would break it down.

Two of the guards on the walkway began firing at the beasts. Reloading their weapons with cold hands, in the wind, was slowing down their next round.

Others saw that the guards had fired at something outside the gate. Soldiers began responding.

Major Smythe and Capitan Dominguez had been standing in the common area. As soon as Smythe realized what was happening, he yelled to Corporal Yardley, "Load your guns with grapeshot! DO IT NOW!"

The stockade shook for a third time. A loud crack was heard as the beam holding the outside world at bay weakened further.

More men had climbed the walkway and had begun firing volley after volley. But the walkway was not completely finished and was not prepared for the weight of so many men and weapons.

Without the necessary supports, the walkway tore away from the stockade pickets and crashed to the ground. Several men were injured.

The second walkway on the southwestern side was empty. Everyone had rushed to shore up the gate in the southeastern edge of the stockade.

The two monsters, that were not employing their shoulders to break the gate, had circled around to the northern wall. They had seen the two extra pickets the previous night.

Each picket would have been needed to be picked up by six to eight men, but the two beasts alone were enough. They maneuvered the pickets up against the fort, creating a steep ramp. Fortunately for the beasts, the logs had not been finished for placement, because they weren't needed.

The unfinished logs provided enough nubs and partial branches to be used as footholds to make the climb easier. The monsters easily went up and over the wall.

Unchallenged, they jumped down off the unfinished walkway and were free to wreak havoc in the fort.

The stockade shook for a fourth time and a crack, louder than the musket fire, rang out. The gate doors exploded inward.

The eight forest devils roared as they saw the opportunity for bloodletting. What they didn't expect was to face two cannons, loaded with grapeshot.

"FIRE!" Yardley yelled, and then a moment later the two cannons boomed. Eight forest devils were shredded as they moved forward.

Almost eighty muskets fired as well, at almost point-blank range. The beasts fell, mostly backwards.

As Smythe and Dominguez moved forward with Lattimore and a few men with fixed bayonets, the screams from the north cut through the night. Most were just recovering their hearing from the percussion of the cannons, and the desperate cries went almost unheard.

Elliott heard them and took two hastily assembled squads in that direction.

The monsters had already killed two soldiers and a civilian woman who was awake and outside because of her curiosity. The monsters had moved into an area of soldiers who were still trying to get themselves dressed. Their weapons were nearby, but not available to them.

The screams began.

Elliott and his armed group arrived. Elliott, seeing the desperate situation, rushed forward, drawing his sword. Stabbing a forest devil in mid-torso, he found himself being lifted off the ground and face to face with the monster.

He felt the monster's free hand on top of his head. Then the beast twisted its hand quickly, breaking Elliott's neck and ending his life.

The monster looked down at the sword protruding from its midsection. It knew its end was near.

The men Elliott had brought with him could not fire, for fear of hitting the Lieutenant. As soon as his dead body hit the ground, they saw the monster look at the sword that protruded from its belly, and they opened fire.

The big creature staggered towards them, reaching forward. It fell forward, jamming the sword out through its back. It was dead.

More screaming. The men reloaded, but others had arrived and ran past them.

More gunfire. The second beast was dispatched.

Dominguez and Smythe were standing over one of the beasts. It lay face up. A large scar ran from the corner of its mouth to its ear.

"Wonder what could have done that to one of these big things?" Smythe asked.

"Sometimes, it is what you don't expect, Major. I had a corporal, one of my missing men actually, that had a similar scar. His drunken father had cut him from mouth to ear with a broken bottle. No war story to brag about. Just a horrible family life. Corporal Jimenez was a good man," the Capitan remembered.

The beast they were standing over moaned and opened its eyes. They both jumped back.

The animal looked at the Spaniard. It squinted and turned its head, seemingly studying the capitan.

Smythe noticed his Spanish counterpart was doing the same thing. It was as if the capitan was studying the animal just as intently.

The monster slowly raised its arm, reaching out for the capitan and then opened its mouth, "Doh-ming-gezzzz."

Smythe, Dominguez and several soldiers heard the animal speak. It was as if time stopped as each witness stood in abject shock at what they had just witnessed.

Dominguez's response, "Jimenez? Is that you?"

The monster was losing strength. Its arm lowered as it looked at the Captain and replied in a raspy voice, "Si, Senor. Soy yo." Then its eyes closed, and its head rolled to the side. It was dead.

"What did he say?" Smythe asked.

A Spanish cavalryman standing behind the Major answered, "Senor Major, he said, 'Yesssir. It is me.'"

The capitan walked away, saying nothing to Smythe. He looked into the face of each of the dead creatures. He searched for some clue that his other men had been changed as well. He found one.

A private that he had commanded bore a purple birthmark that covered a third of his forehead and a few inches down by his left eye, almost to his cheek. He found one of the creatures with the same facial mark.

It was not unusual for the Spanish army or cavalry to have a good number of members with unsightly scars and deformities. When a man felt that he couldn't cope within polite society, he joined the military to find worth and to hide from the world.

Dominguez was convinced that the natives had finally used their black magic. They made monsters out of good men. And he hated them for it.

The imminent planned attack was just what he needed to exact his revenge.

Chapter 15

The Counter Attack

Ten of the beasts were killed. The cannons filled with grapeshot were obviously the single most effective defense that could have been employed. Soldiers and citizens were congratulating Smythe for his quick thinking.

Grammy was chief among those with laudatory comments and a grateful attitude. She knew that had ten of those monsters been set loose inside the walls of the village, many people would have died.

It seemed odd that they never had attacked so aggressively with that many before. They had seen almost fifteen at one time before, but some had stayed back at the tree line while five or six would swoop in and attack. Then the attackers would return to the tree line, and five or six more would attack.

It was during that attack, where they had seen so many, that they lost thirty-one settlers. The beasts used that tactic for over two hours. It was why she insisted that a stockade be built as soon as she was put in charge. It should have been done much sooner.

Another unique aspect of this attack was that it was at night. This was the second night encounter, but the first was just to kill the beast they had trapped in the hole. It wasn't an attack against the settlement, as much as it was a mission to assassinate the captured forest devil.

In light of what she had just been told her by Capitan Dominguez, were they just trying to silence the beast? Was it one of his men? Would it have eventually spoken?

She put her musings aside and ordered the gate be immediately rebuilt and fortified. The men jumped right on it. The logs on the north side were discovered and used in the repairs.

Those not repairing the damage continued to prepare for the counterattack, which was moved to the following night. It was assumed that the Indians did not know that the whites knew their secret and would not be expecting a retaliatory strike.

At first light, many of the American and Spanish soldiers and quite a few of the villagers who weren't working on the gate, gathered at the cemetery. Grammy had been correct. Smythe would use this sacred plot of ground to bury some of his own men.

When the final tally was completed, seven soldiers and two villagers had been killed by the beasts that had snuck over the wall. A few soldiers had injuries, but they were minor.

It was painful for Smythe to lose men, but losing Elliott was an extremely hard blow to process. He died trying to save his men. Some of the soldiers even wept openly at his graveside.

No Spaniards were killed, unless you counted the transformed beasts. Regardless, Dominguez was by Smythe's side lending support during the memorial and graveside service.

Pastor Maurice Hamilton, a Moravian clergyman, did the honors. He was the preacher at the church that had been built. Many of the settlers had no clue what a Moravian was, but they believed in Jesus, and that was what counted.

When it was over, Smythe suggested to the Spanish Captain that he have a burial service for his two men that died as transformed forest devils. Dominguez refused. He believed they were his men, but the forest devils were still the enemy, and he couldn't honor their passing because of it.

Smythe liked Dominguez. The man was principled. Having not dealt with Spaniards before, Dominguez was making the Major think very highly of them.

Grammy had been standing nearby the Major and the Captain during the memorial service. She witnessed their interaction She too was finding herself becoming fond of Dominguez.

She wondered why she had spent so much effort keeping the Spaniards at arm's length whenever they stopped by. Had she been more hospitable, they could have stuck around and provided a sense of security while they built the stockade.

She was sad, knowing that Capitan Dominguez and his men would soon be gone. And she was quite concerned about what the French might send in their place.

The graveside services ended. Everyone returned to the safety of the stockade. Tonight, the fighting men would attack the Indians, and hopefully kill any forest devils that were still alive.

At 12:00 a.m. Major Smythe sent Ranger Sergeant Camden and his rangers to do a complete inspection of the tree lines surrounding the stockade. The Major didn't want any more surprises.

Camden and the other seven rangers returned at 12:50 a.m. and reported that all was clear. At 1:00 a.m. the gates opened and the march on the native camp began as scheduled.

The Army men were the first out of the stockade, followed by the cannons and then the Spanish cavalry. The militia brought up the rear.

The plan was finally coming together, and the men were ready. They were aided by a full moon.

The rangers had guessed that it would take about three hours to march on the village. They were correct.

At 4:15 a.m. the military procession had reached the western edge of the village. As the cannons were being set up, the Spanish cavalry got into position.

The militia circled around to the eastern end of the native encampment. No one was stirring.

The rangers had gone ahead and killed two natives that were on watch duty. The Indian sentries had become complacent and were sitting around a fire on the southern edge of the native village.

Eliminating them had been very easy for Camden and his men. No one had stirred since. No relief for the native sentries had arrived.

Corporal Yardley reported to Smythe that the cannons were ready. It was time for the plan to commence.

A lanyard was pulled to engage the friction primer. A loud boom was heard as the first round flew and hit its mark. A corner section of the lodge tore away.

The second, third and fourth cannons were fired. Two rounds missed their mark slightly, and the fourth was a direct hit, forming a large hole in the lodge.

The reloading was a frenzied affair. The cannons needed to re-fire quickly, before the Indians and their beasts could muster a response.

Corrections were made in the trajectories and four more shots were fired, almost in unison. The lodge collapsed and flew away towards the west end of the village.

At the last minute, Smythe had sent the rangers up onto the rocks to act as snipers. The rangers had custom-made rifled muskets. The weapons were truly a rarity and were being painstakingly produced one at a time by a German gunsmith in Philadelphia.

The American Army purchased some for a few ranger units. They were not able to be mass-produced, but what the German gunsmith could make were immediately snatched up by the military. Camden's group was the second group to receive them.

The rifling made the muskets many times more accurate than the common gun of the day. Smythe had been treated to a demonstration of their accuracy almost a year previously. The Major, in effect, was the first to employ snipers during an engagement.

Camden and his men took to the high ground and were thrilled at their assignment.

The Army was to hold back until the cannons had targeted the cave entrance a few times. Once Smythe gave orders for the infantry to move in, the cannons were supposed to be primed with grapeshot, for self-defense.

The cave entrance was clearly visible. Four more targeted volleys hit the gaping hole in the ground. By this time, so much more was occurring.

After the first volley, the natives desperately tried to recover from slumber. Their appearance around their teepees and small lodges was at first a trickle. After the second volley, they poured out of their homes.

The rangers were enjoying felling them as they appeared. The rifles were being employed in a most accurate and expert manner.

The natives were trying to group themselves together for a counterassault in the direction of the cannons. They obviously saw the opportunity to circle around the cannons from the south.

Their attempts were met by the Spanish cavalry, which cut them down quietly with lance and sword. They never found it necessary to use their short muskets or pistols. Not a shot was fired from the Spaniards.

Women, children and the elderly were being hurried westward out of the other end of the village. They were unaware of the militia's presence until they began to fall.

Lieutenant Turner, the silversmith, yelled "FIRE!" at his first rank. They were broken into four ranks of fifteen each.

Eleven Indians fell.

The same order was given to the second rank and then the third and fourth. The first was reloaded and ready to go.

After all four ranks had fired twice, thirty-nine non-combatants lay dead or dying. Several had escaped through a gap that headed southwest.

Turner ordered Sergeants Matthew and Luke Bannister to take their squads and hunt them down. The Lieutenant took the rest of the men and moved forward into the village.

Everything was working perfectly.

Smythe finally ordered the infantry forward. There were a few minor skirmishes, but the natives had lost their will to fight. Many were executed where they stood.

It was Lattimore who returned to the Major and asked, "Where are the beasts, sir?"

Smythe had already run that question through his own mind. He didn't like the options that he was imagining.

"Sergeant Lattimore, make and light torches and take first platoon into the cave. Station second platoon around the entrance. Assemble third platoon and send them back to the settlement with the militia, just in case."

"And fourth platoon, sir?" Lattimore asked.

"They'll stay here and guard the cannons."

Capitan Dominguez rode up behind Smythe as he was issuing his orders. "What are you thinking, Major Smythe?"

"I'm thinking that we haven't seen the chief or his medicine men. Ranger Camden had told me they stand out quite a bit because of their attire. Did you see them? You know exactly what they look like."

"Si, Senor Major. They are not here, as far as what I've seen."

"That leaves three options. They are hiding in the cave with the beasts. They are hiding in the woods with the forest devils, or they are attacking the settlement as we waste our time here."

"My men and I will make the best time on horseback. We will leave immediately, if you wish," Dominguez offered.

"Yes, Captain. Head back to the settlement, and we will handle the other possibilities here," Smythe said, gratefully accepting his offer.

"Do you still want third platoon to head back as well?" Lattimore asked after Dominguez rode off.

"Absolutely. His cavalry unit may do some good, but if there are too many of the beasts, they won't last long," Smythe explained.

Chapter 16

Down into the Pit

Lattimore and his men searched throughout the village and found sufficient tallow, which the Indians used in soapmaking and lamp fuel, to make the torches needed for illumination in the cave.

Sergeant Lattimore was a brave soldier. He had seen action at the tail end of the Revolution and several Indian campaigns. Not much frightened the seasoned soldier.

This situation had him fighting his fear constantly. He knew he could best another human being in combat. He had done it many times, but these were monsters who seemed many times bigger and stronger than men.

The only comforting thing that he knew about them was that they could be killed. At least that was cause for hope.

First platoon spent almost an hour making torches. They would descend into the lightless hole with one third of the torches lit. Tallow burned slow and steady. When the first torches burned out, then the second wave would be lit and then the third. The third would be used as the unit moved quickly back out into the light of day. No one wished to be caught in the lightless underworld that awaited them.

Lattimore asked Camden and his rangers to take point going into the cave. If the creatures were in the cave, this request was suicide.

It was no secret that First Sergeant Lattimore was jealous of the rangers, Camden in particular. Camden could have protested, or even made a logical argument for them to not go in first. But he accepted the request because he didn't want to give the First Sergeant the satisfaction of seeing him and his men backing out of the assignment.

Three of the rangers grabbed and lit their torches. The other five rangers grabbed unlit torches and carried them sticking out from their rucksacks.

The elite unit moved into the darkened entranceway and then disappeared. Lattimore sent five men to shadow the rangers, and then he entered the cave with the balance of first platoon following.

There was a cool breeze coming up from below. The feel of it was refreshing. The smell of it was sickening.

Stench was the most appropriate word. One of the rangers turned to Camden and asked, "Damn, Sergeant Camden! Is that skunk shit?"

"How the hell would I know? Stop talking and keep your eyes open!"

Camden was in no mood for chit chat as they stepped ever closer to their own doom. He was sure the smell was confirming the presence of the beasts.

Dominguez was pushing his men and their horses. He didn't want anything to happen to Grammy or her people on his watch, even though his watch was officially over.

To him, his continued presence required that he continue to do his job. He knew the American infantry would be behind him and ready to do their job as well.

Even at a fast pace, the infantry would take three hours to arrive back at Thornside. His cavalry should reach the settlement in forty minutes. He secretly hoped the beasts were there. The capitan wanted to kill them. All of them.

The time passed quickly, and he and his horse soldiers burst from the northern tree line and into the field. He saw guards up on the walkways. Nothing looked amiss.

They arrived at the gates as they were being opened. Grammy had been called at the first sight of them.

"What is wrong, Captain? Where is the infantry?"

He dismounted and filled her in on what had happened during the attack.

She responded, "So the beasts are missing. Maybe they are still on their way. Get your men inside, and we'll rustle up some food." She then alerted her lookouts to be especially mindful.

Over two hours later, the infantry platoon and the entire militia arrived back at the settlement and were fed as well. Still no beasts had shown themselves.

"What do you think, Captain? What is going on?" Grammy asked.

"Senora, Grammy, we either killed them all, the other night, or they are still back with Major Smythe. And unfortunately, our forces are split. Now that you have the American Army platoon and the entire militia here, I and my men are heading back."

Less than twenty minutes later, the Spanish cavalry was heading out the gate, to return to what had been the native village. Capitan Dominguez had no intention of waiting around.

He knew they had killed ten beasts during the attack on the settlement. Did the Indians have many more than that?

If the Indians had any military sense or cunning, they wouldn't have risked their entire forest devil contingent on one attack. Although, he was sure that they never anticipated Major Smythe's coup with the cannons loaded with grapeshot.

That one genius move ended the lives of eight of the beasts. Had they snuck a few more over the north wall, the outcome could have been tragic.

Sergeant Garcia rode up alongside the Capitan, "Capitan Dominguez, it is my pleasure to serve under your command."

"But what, Sergeant? I know there is a but coming," Dominguez responded.

"But, Senor, your obligation here is over. We could head to New Orleans and board a ship, and no one would fault you for it. You have served admirably and faithfully. You have even upheld a great deal of goodwill towards these Americans."

"They stole the humanity of seven of my men. And subsequently, those men have lost their lives. Or at least I know that to be true for at least two of them. The rest I have assumed. The chief and the medicine men have to be stopped. They are responsible.

As the two men conversed, five of the seven remaining forest devils stalked them. The other two devils were waiting back in their cave home, alone with no one to control their actions.

The chief and the five shamans, were riding on horseback behind the Spaniards. They had sent the five devils ahead to ambush the cavalry.

The beasts totally unnerved the horses that were not used to them. The Spaniards were starting to have trouble with their steeds as the creatures moved in.

The cavalrymen were noticing their horses were becoming increasingly agitated. They were slowing down in an area where the forest floor was littered with jagged rocks the size of small cannonballs.

It was a stretch of about one hundred yards and the horses could not move as swiftly through that terrain. It was a perfect place for the forest devils to strike.

And they did.

Dominguez yelled out to his men, "Slow it down! It's that rocky place we experienced twice before. Take care of your animals!"

Everyone pulled up a bit and were happy to do so as their horses became increasingly more squirrelly.

Jumping from the shadows, the devils knocked four riders off their horses and onto the treacherously rocky ground.

The men were too bunched up to use their lances and Dominguez knew it, "Drop your lances! Pistols and swords!" he ordered. The men, having been well trained, did as they were told.

Two more riders were knocked to the ground, but several pistols were fired, and the giants screeched and screamed. Swords slashed and one huge animal fell.

A few more shots from pistols and short muskets felled a second beast. Three more riders were taken down. Five of the unmounted men were dead. Two were badly wounded and two were using their swords to slash at their enemy.

Dominguez, who did not carry a lance, saw one of the spears stuck in the ground. He quickly galloped over to where it was, reached down and picked it up.

He continued on to an animal that had its back to him. He rode on and drove his lance through the beast as it was being slashed by a cavalryman on the ground. The man was grateful as the creature slumped and fell on its side.

Dominguez pulled his pistol and shot one of the two remaining beasts. The ball parted the hair on the beast's left shoulder, but now its entire attention was on Dominguez.

It lunged and the capitan's horse reared up, throwing him off and onto to the stony ground where he struck his head on a large rock. The world went black.

The remaining cavalrymen, that included Sergeant Garcia, chased off the two remaining forest devils. The one, the capitan had shot, stopped and turned and hissed. It picked up a rock and threw it, hitting a cavalryman and knocking him off his horse.

The rest of the men dismounted, reloaded, set up a defensive perimeter and began to attend to their wounded. Garcia sought out Dominguez. The Capitan was still unconscious, which was the reason he was still alive.

Had he remained able to defend himself, the wounded beast was prepared to destroy him. The current twisted workings of its mind blamed the humans for its current circumstances.

Dominguez returned to consciousness with a headache and a bump at the back of his head. Garcia took temporary command and insisted on taking the dead and wounded back to the settlement.

Dominguez was in no condition to argue.

Chapter 17

The Encounter

The men had been walking for a surprisingly long time. Camden was becoming more tense with every step, which was a shared condition with every man in the cave. The first set of torches were about to go out.

One by one, the lights faded and went out, as the new wave of illumination was employed. In the waning light of the first round of tallow torches, a narrow passageway was missed.

The two cave dwellers, that had been left behind, were hidden in the crevasse. As the last men passed by, the devils pounced.

They knocked several men to the ground. One of the monsters snatched a torch, that had been recently lit, and threw it at the men heading into the cave.

Chaos reigned for the next few moments as the enraged brutes knocked men to the floor of the cave and stomped them with their large, heavy feet.

Two more torches were tossed at the men who were turning to defend themselves. In the seemingly lightless environment, the devils had good eyesight. The torches, as much as they helped the men see, were a hindrance to the devils.

The beasts headed away from the men and ran upward towards the cave entrance.

Gunshots rang out behind them and echoed off the cave walls. The forest devils moved at incredible speed and somehow avoided being hit.

The men of platoon two, at the cave entrance, heard the faint sound of gunfire and took up their arms in preparation for whatever might emerge from the dark hole.

They waited for almost twenty minutes. The huge bipeds finally emerged into the light at great speed.

A sergeant yelled, "FIRE!"

The immediate area was filled with the deafening sound of gunfire from more than forty guns. Visibility became a problem, as the smoke from those same guns drifted towards the cave entrance.

When the smoke had cleared, one animal lay dead on the ground. It had been the lead beast and had taken the brunt of the volley.

The second beast was nowhere in sight.

The beast had taken five hits, but not to vital organs or arteries. He and the other devil had burst out of the cave at a high rate of speed. He was the second out and was shielded from the vast majority of the incoming musket balls.

The pain he was feeling, from his own wounds, couldn't compare to the agony of being able to remember his time as a human being. That gnawing pain is what made him hate them so much. They were still human.

He and the others, that had been made to resemble the original beasts which were natural freaks of nature, hated the natives as well. But the chief and the medicine men held a great power over them, which prevented the monsters from seeking revenge against them.

He wanted death, either theirs or his own, but he was afraid to die in this condition. Would hell await him, or was this it? No torment could be worse than what he was already feeling.

The fragment of himself that was still human wanted revenge against everyone. But returning to the native village would be insanity.

He stopped and sniffed the air. Two of his tormented kind were nearby. He could tell by their scent that they were two of the females.

The native maidens, used for the sacrifice, were never killed. They had been turned. That had always been Mi Soke's plan. The maidens were the females that he needed to experiment as to whether the ste-te sh'a ta-ka could reproduce naturally. Over time, some progress had been made. After some stillbirths and a few deaths during childbirth, some live births occurred. He always killed the pups, which is what he called them. For now, he wanted his monsters to have no distractions.

The beasts burned with rage over Mi Soke's treatment of their offspring, but his magic was too powerful for them to do anything about it. Every year, another maiden was turned. It was only a matter of time before the beasts reproduced and passed on their traits naturally.

The wounded beast from the cave, in his former life, was known as Diego Montagne. He was a Corporal in the Spanish cavalry. He had a wife and children back in the motherland, beautiful Espana. His heart yearned for what would never be again.

He must find the females. Maybe together they could attack the humans.

His wounds were painful and throbbed incessantly as he tried to formulate a plan.

He sniffed the air again. The chief of the natives and his henchman were with the other two.

Pain. He felt a freedom that he had not felt before. He didn't feel the oppressive fingers of his captors clouding his mind. Was his pain breaking that connection?

And then he knew. He would ambush the native leaders and kill them as quickly as he could. He had felt hatred for them before, but this was the first time that he felt he could do something about it.

Pain racked his body once again, only this time he welcomed it.

Pain was freedom.

The rangers and first platoon exited the cave. Camden noticed the dead beast, but he knew there had been more than one.

He asked the Sergeant commanding second platoon what he had seen. The Sergeant confirmed that two beasts had exited the cave.

Camden and the rangers began looking for the trail the escaped creature had made. Smythe had heard the gunfire and arrived at the cave entrance.

Lattimore filled the Major in on the encounter in the tunnel. Smythe's first question was, "Casualties?" Just one word, and Lattimore knew he was in trouble.

"I don't know, sir. We gave chase, after it was apparent the forest devils were escaping. I am sure we had some casualties," he admitted.

"I will take up the chase with second platoon, Lattimore. Go back in and retrieve your dead and injured. That should have been your first priority. Right now, your injured men are lying in the boughs of a darkened cave. Get to it."

Lattimore's ears burned as he stood and accepted being scolded by the Major. The worst part was that Smythe was absolutely in the right. He had lost his head over wanting to kill the beasts more than anything else. He had neglected his duties. He had left men behind. Shame filled him.

Lattimore wasted no time in returning to the cave entrance. He did a quick inventory of the torches available and determined they had enough to retrieve the dead and injured. It bothered him further that he had no idea of how many of each they would find.

Four members of each platoon were designated as stretcher bearers. As such, they carried the poles and canvas support needed to assemble the medical transport.

Smythe sent second platoon's stretcher bearers to help, making a total of eight. Lattimore hoped they wouldn't need all of them.

They reentered the cave, and it struck Lattimore that just because two beasts made themselves known, that didn't mean there weren't more down below.

He stopped and shared the thought with his men.

"Stay alert, men. This may not be over."

They moved more quickly than the earlier descent. Lattimore just wanted to retrieve his men and get the hell out. That was his exact thought.

Forty minutes later, they found the point of attack.

Two men lay dead. Three were injured.

All five were loaded on stretchers and carried out.

The two dead men would be buried in the woods with the other seven men who had died in the attack on the native village.

The three injured men would accompany the eight injured during the village incursion. They would return to the settlement with fourth platoon and the cannons.

Lattimore sent his scouts to find which way Smythe and second platoon had headed. He needed to back up the Major and his men.

That was the right thing to do. The First Sergeant needed to get back on track and make good decisions based on sound military experience.

It was the only reasonable way to cast off the shame that he felt.

Chapter 18

The Attack on Mi Soke

The monster, that had been Diego Montagne in his former life, stalked the other two beasts, along with Chief Mi Soke and his five medicine men. If the other two forest devils were aware of Diego, they did not show it.

Diego had tried to stay downwind as much as possible, but he wasn't doing a great job of it. His tortured mind still maintained the intellectual capacity of a human. He wondered if the other two beasts were intuitive enough to know what he was doing and allowing it to happen.

He was close enough to see them. The native leader and his men were riding mules. They preferred them for being more sure-footed in the forest, easier to feed and able to bear greater loads when needed.

They traded for them when possible. The natives did not keep the necessary herds of horses and donkeys around to produce them. The Arkansas Post had them available quite often, as they were castoff by trappers passing through.

And although mules could be stubborn, they weren't as skittish as horses when around the forest devils. Mi Soke didn't care about any of that. They were something to ride to keep up with the monsters he created.

The first forest devils he had encountered were natural. They were a primitive form of man that had not gone the way of extinction.

They were naturally smarter than the other mammals, but not as intelligent as modern man. Using the black arts that he practiced regularly, he found a common link in its makeup that he could exploit.

The magic made the science of it unimportant. He was able to make men into monsters by mixing the blood of the original animals with a combination of natural elements. He concocted a monster-making drink.

Eventually, the original animals died, but Mi Soke had enough of their dried blood to repeat the process many more times. Thunder Tongue had made him a powerful master of the black arts.

The liberated, but wounded, forest devil caught a glimpse of the chief and his men. They were following an old deer trail through the forest.

Diego did something the bewitched beasts did not do well. He climbed a tree. It was perfect for bearing his great weight, and if they continued on the deer run, they would pass underneath him.

And as expected, the natives stayed on the deer trail. The moment of truth regarding the two beasts that walked ahead of them was coming to bear.

They walked under Diego without a reaction of any kind. Their nonchalance was purposeful. They would have felt his presence and definitely would have smelled him. Diego guessed they were counting on his success.

The natives rode single file. Three medicine men rode ahead of Mi Soke and two rode behind him. Diego knew the chief had to die first.

As the native leader rode under him, he dropped down without a sound. He landed on the native chief and his mule with all his seven hundred and seventy pounds.

Mi Soke died quickly as his clavicle broke, his shoulders collapsed and his broken ribs entered his lungs. Considering his connection to the evil spirits, he died unceremoniously under the crushing weight of the beast.

The mule under Mi Soke broke a foreleg and toppled over on his side, braying and squealing. The male forest devil had no interest in doing the mule any additional harm. His attention was focused on regaining his own footing after the beast had broken his fall and softened his landing.

Diego turned to the two shamans in the rear. He quickly knocked them off their mules and stomped them into the next life.

The three medicine men in front were turning around with some difficulty because of the narrowness of the trail. Their mules were not cooperating.

The two female forest devils, inspired by Diego's actions, pulled the medicine men off their horses, and Diego worked his way to the front of their line to finish them.

When he was done, the three of them looked at the carnage from the attack. The mules ran off, with the exception of the one with the broken leg.

Diego returned to that animal with a large, heavy rock and put the creature out of its misery. It was motivated by the memory of compassion that had once been part of Diego's humanity.

Ultimately, they were animals. Once freed from their Indian oppressors, they quickly reverted to typical animal behavior.

While under the native's dominance, they were not allowed to mate, except when Mi Soke was experimenting. Mi Soke preferred to create the monsters through supernatural means. It was possible that naturally born forest devils may not have been under his control.

Here at the site of their rebellion, Diego took turns holding each female down as he expressed his dominance through the reproductive process.

It couldn't have been described as rape, for both females were willing. They began to give themselves over to natural mammalian behavior.

With the spells broken, their humanity slipped farther away. Their thoughts turned to survival as they escaped into the woods.

The rangers had picked up and followed the trail. After over four hours, they came across the dead natives and the mule. They waited for Smythe and second platoon to catch up.

When Smythe and his men arrived, first platoon had already joined them. The Major was shown the results of the forest devils' rebellion.

"How many of the beasts do you figure are left, by what you are observing?"

"Three, sir," Camden responded. "One is a giant, and the other two are slightly smaller."

"Only three of the monsters left. The Indians are all dead. Let's return to the settlement and see what happens as time progresses," Smythe said.

"Sir, we aren't that far behind them. We could finish them off," Camden suggested hopefully.

"Sergeant, we have enough light to get back to the safety of the stockade. I don't plan on losing any more men over these beasts."

The Army headed through the forest in the direction of the settlement.

Chapter 19

The Spaniards

When Smythe and his men returned, they found that the Spanish cavalry had tried to return to the village to render assistance and came under attack. He learned that five of the men died. Their loyalty to the mission, and to their new American friends, had cost them the ultimate price. They could have been headed to New Orleans instead.

Dominguez and his wounded men were still bedridden. Dominguez was recovering from a concussion. His daily headaches stayed with him for weeks.

During those weeks, Smythe and Dominguez became fast friends. Eventually, after the winter months passed, it became time for the Spanish cavalry to head homeward.

The gates were opened and the streets were lined by Smythe and his soldiers standing at attention as a sign of respect for their Spanish friends.

Grammy and the entire village turned out as well. They loaded the Spanish down with jerky and other food stuffs to get them safely to their destination.

Dominguez saluted his American counterpart and exited the stockade. His men paraded behind him.

The townspeople clapped and cheered.

The Spanish cavalry had ended their tour in the Louisiana Territory. It was time to return to Espana.

During their weeks of recovery, there were no Indians to contend with, and on a better note, no forest devils made themselves known.

Almost four weeks after Dominguez and his men departed, a column of American heavy dragoons came up from the south. They were a dragoon unit left over from when such units were first formed during the War of Independence.

The cavalry designation in the American military machine was just beginning and the dragoons, who were simply mounted infantry, were being phased out. Their horses were simply a means to convey them to a place where they could dismount and fight as infantrymen.

The actual cavalry, recently formed, was taking on more specific training in horsemanship, close quarter weapons training, tactics and maneuverability in combat. The days of the dragoons were waning.

Captain Sylvester Berkstresser commanded the seventy-three men that followed him into the settlement. Their arrival was pushing the town of Thornside to its maximum capacity.

After the introductions, Berkstresser handed Smythe a letter from Washington. In it, Smythe read that he and his men were being relieved to return to Washington, under the condition that the Indians and the purported forest monsters that had plagued the settlement had been eliminated.

They, of course, had and Smythe was relieved. He immediately shared the news with Lattimore and the rest of the command. Hoots and hollers were heard throughout the assembly.

Tonight would be a celebration. Beer was being successfully produced and would be flowing in abundance.

Smythe and Grammy invited Berkstresser and his officers to enjoy dinner with them at the meeting house. Lattimore and Lieutenant Turner would be in attendance as well.

At the dinner that evening, Berkstresser was asked to regale them with their exploits from Washington to the Louisiana Territory. He informed them that their assumptions were incorrect.

He had received his orders, not in Washington, but Savannah, Georgia. His orders first sent him to New Orleans to make sure that the Spanish presence was gone.

Apparently, Washington had heard of some resistance from the Spanish occupiers. France had requested assistance from the newly formed United States to rid the territory of those who were refusing to leave.

Smythe asked, "Why would our nation help France against another European power? What's in it for us?"

"I hesitate to talk out of turn," Berkstresser began, "but the territory will soon be ours. A deal with France is in the works. We are to treat this land as our own."

"And did you find any Spanish resistance?" Grammy asked.

"Yes. Sadly we lost eight men in a battle with a Spanish cavalry unit, just outside of New Orleans. They fought like they were possessed. But don't fear, we killed every last one of them."

Smythe looked at Grammy, Lattimore and Turner. They knew it had to be Dominguez and his men returning to New Orleans. There was no way Dominguez would have engaged in a battle unless defending himself.

The worst part was knowing the reason for the delay of their departure. It was because they stayed to help their American friends. Smythe felt physically ill.

Grammy and the other two weren't faring well either.

"Have I said something to upset you?" Berkstresser asked.

"How many cavalrymen were in that Spanish unit, sir?" Lattimore asked.

"About twenty-five or so. Why is that important?" the Captain asked.

"Did you get to talk to the commanding officer?" Smythe queried.

"If you must know, yes. He claimed he had helped the American Army kill Indians and monsters. Can you imagine? Monsters of all things. He sounded like a crazy man. So having just lost eight men in that fight, I shot him in the head to end the encounter. I take my orders very seriously."

"Excuse me, please,' Smythe said as he stood and left the room.

"What is going on here?" Berkstresser demanded.

"You killed our friends! We were, in fact, fighting Indians and monsters, just as he said. They could have left many months ago, but they stayed to help us. You killed them, damn you!"

"Major Smythe is an unhappy man, as are the rest of us who had fought alongside them," Grammy explained with deep sadness in her voice.

"But monsters? You expect me to believe in fairytales? I am at a loss for what to think," Berkstresser stated.

"Show him, Sergeant Lattimore," Grammy requested.

"Follow me, sir," the Sergeant invited, with sadness coloring his voice and demeanor as well.

Berkstresser stood and followed him to the back of the room. Berkstresser's Lieutenant and First Sergeant trailed behind the two men, to observe. A large, specially built cabinet had been made with two tall doors.

What was about to be revealed was made possible by one of the settlers named Lars Janssen. He had learned an interesting craft in Holland, his motherland. It was just becoming an art form in America. Lars was a skilled taxidermist.

To preserve part of the settlement's history, it was suggested to preserve one of the monsters. So, Mr. Janssen did just that.

Lattimore opened the large double doors.

Berkstresser stepped back, while placing his hand on the hilt of his sword. It took a moment for him to realize that it wasn't alive.

He then stepped forward and examined the creature from head to toe. He stepped even closer, sniffed it and made a sour face.

Grammy had walked up behind him, "Dead or alive, the damn things smell horrible. Maybe they started as skunks?

Who the hell knows? But they're real, Captain Berkstresser. And those Spaniards you slaughtered helped us fight them and the Indians. They earned our respect and our friendship. And ain't no way in hell they would have fought you unless you gave them no choice."

There. She said it. It didn't assuage her grief, but it lessened her anger a notch. The truth had been spoken. If this Captain was going to take Smythe's place, he needed to know who she was.

At first, Berkstresser didn't react, except to continue staring at the monster in the cabinet.

"You are right, Miss Hillburn. We fired first. We saw the Spanish flag and had been convinced, ahead of time, that the remaining Spaniards would be hostile. They fought valiantly, if it's any consolation."

"It ain't," she replied. "I'll be retiring now, Captain. See you in the morning."

"Good night, Miss Hillburn."

"Let's get something straight. I'm Grammy. Plain and simple. Miss Hillburn faded away to nothin' a long time ago."

"Okay, Grammy. I am very sorry about your friends."

She walked out without saying another word.

Lattimore closed and locked the cabinet.

"Any of those left, Sergeant?" Berkstresser asked.

"Sir, as far as we know, there are three. Haven't seen them for five or six months. As far as the hostile Indians, we killed all the Quapaw that lived in this area. At least all the ones that followed Chief Mi Soke. They was the bad ones. We killed every man, woman and child. Don't feel great about that, but it was necessary."

"Do you think the monsters are gone for good?"

"They have never been this quiet since we have been here. I think the Indians controlled them. Now, no Indians. I think they ran off to be wild animals. Just don't let your guard down," Lattimore advised. "Good night, Captain."

He walked out with Turner, who hadn't said a single word all night. He too had befriended many of the Spaniards and had even made them a few special silver trinkets for loved ones back in Spain.

Berkstresser, his Lieutenant and First Sergeant sat alone by the fire. The meeting house was where the three were sleeping on their first night.

And it was an evening of deep reflection. Things weren't always what they seemed. Berkstresser felt horrible for what he had done.

He executed the Spanish commander for telling the truth. All this because he believed in Washington's infallibility, and because he didn't believe in monsters.

And he wondered if he didn't hold a deep-seated prejudice against non-English speaking people. He almost laughed since he was only a third-generation citizen of the New World, as some still called it, from a German family. His parents spoke heavily accented English and his grandparents in Philadelphia spoke a broken immigrant English.

He had known some prejudice as a child, as some accused him of being a little Hessian spy. But none of those people had shot him to death as he did the Spanish Captain.

Before meeting these people, he struggled with what he had done, but justified it as an act of war. Washington said the remaining Spaniards were hostiles and trespassers on what would soon become American soil.

He was amazed at what a man could justify. He no longer had that luxury and fell into fervent prayer as soon as he determined his Lieutenant and First Sergeant were asleep.

Chapter 20

The Transition

Berkstresser's men had talked to Smythe's soldiers and many townspeople about their travels. The encounter with the Spanish cavalry was repeated time and again.

It caused much grief and consternation and a few fights broke out, mostly between the soldiers. Lattimore and Berkstresser's top noncommissioned officer quelled the discord. But they couldn't erase the grief.

Smythe and his men didn't leave straightaway. They needed to produce the necessary provisions to aid in their travels.

The cobbler and his apprentice helped to repair the footwear of quite a few dozen soldiers. Without the repairs, their shoes would not have lasted through the long march returning them back east.

Several of the local ladies also chipped in to help with uniform repairs. Smythe did not want his men arriving home in disarray.

It turned out that Captain Berkstresser was a good man. Where the Spaniards were concerned, he listened to the reports from Washington instead of trusting his own instincts. He was not a bloodthirsty monster.

He apologized more than enough times to Major Smythe. And the senior officer finally let him off the hook and accepted his remorseful plea. The man was truly repentant and was being harder on himself than anyone else could have been.

Once a good rapport was established between the two commanders, the combined units worked at expanding the settlement and making it into a fort with the settlement remaining inside. They officially named it Fort Dominguez.

The town would remain inside the fort and would continue to be called Thornside.

The project added three weeks to Smythe's stay, but that time was needed for his command to become travel worthy. It worked out well for all concerned.

Many settlers had built up the courage to inhabit their claims. During the daytime, those who weren't helping to expand the fort were building small cabins on their frontier land claims.

By the time Smythe and his men were ready to leave, a third of the town's population had vacated the stockade and were living on their own lands. The American frontier was expanding, prior to it actually belonging to the United States.

Grammy remained the leader of the civilians and was slowly establishing a rapport with Berkstresser. It was made easier when Smythe forgave him for his overzealous blunder. She then felt that she, too, could put it behind her.

On the night before Smythe and his men were prepared to leave, he gifted Captain Berkstresser with the caissons and the four cannons. He felt confident that Washington would approve.

Berkstresser began to mentally work on a design for better ramparts to hold cannon emplacements in the fort. But first he needed to give Smythe and his men a decent send off.

They celebrated all evening. Alcohol, however, was off the menu. There was nothing but fresh meat, soups and breads. Smythe called these good marching foods.

The next morning, the gates were opened and Smythe made his rounds to say goodbye. His last goodbye was Grammy Hillburn. It was the longest hug for which he could remember being a part.

"If I were younger, or you were older, I wouldn't let you leave, Reginald Smythe. I guess we'll just have to wonder what it would have been like if either one of us was the right age," she cackled and smiled.

Smythe laughed as well. He had really developed a fondness for the woman. He wanted to say something like, she was like a second mom, or a favorite aunt, but he knew that wouldn't be what she wanted to hear.

He kissed her on the cheek and said, "Goodbye, Grammy." And then he mounted his steed and slowly trotted through the gate.

Lattimore gave the command to move out, and the men began the long trek back to Washington.

Some of the women that had traveled west with Smythe stayed behind. This was their new home. Constance followed Smythe.

She had never given in to prostituting herself. As far as anyone was concerned, she and Smythe were still an item so the men avoided her. Smythe found out about her faithfulness and was grateful.

Two months passed and Captain Berkstresser had established regular routine patrols along the frontier area where the homesteads were popping up. His priority was to keep the peace in the territory that he was assigned to command.

A few additional groups of people with Spanish land grants showed up and claimed their stake in the area. The homestead region was becoming a large area to cover.

Hundreds of homesteaders had erected small cabins, separate summer kitchens, barns, smokehouses and miles and miles of fencing. Some of the wealthier arrivals had slaves and erected slave quarters. The area was booming.

The dragoons were not only the military presence in the area, but also the law. For now, Berkstresser and his men were following a translation of a French code of conduct, to ensure the legality of their actions. It was rather vague in areas.

For lack of a better way to handle matters, Berkstresser made Grammy Hillburn the magistrate for the northern

Louisiana Territory. He wasn't sure if he had the authority to do so, but there was no one to say otherwise.

He had his men, and a few locals, construct a jail with dormitories that featured bars on the windows. It was similar to one that Berkstresser had seen in Savannah.

There was very little need for the jail or Grammy's services. Life on the frontier was becoming idyllic. No Indians. No outlaws to speak of. Just neighbor helping neighbor.

But most good things must come to an end. This was no exception.

One day, a patrol returned, and the Sergeant in charge stood before the Captain and Grammy sat in the corner to listen in. She held quite a bit of clout, even among the soldiers.

"Sir," the Sergeant began, "we did our usual patrol. All was well until we got to the Spencer homestead." The man stopped for dramatic effect or for permission to continue. It was anyone's guess.

"Don't make me drag the report from your lips, Sergeant. Get on with it."

"The Spencers were gone, sir. And then the Campbells, the Washburns, the Tanners and the Millers. Five homesteads were abandoned. But it wasn't natural."

"Explain," the Captain sighed.

"There was blood in the barn at the Spencer place. At the Campbells, there wasn't any blood, but their dinner was on the table, like they had just vanished before they could eat it.

"The Washburn's front door was cleaved in two. It was a very heavy door, like most cabins have in that area. At the Tanners, there was blood inside the house. And at the Millers, we found a musket that was broken in two. It had been fired. We saw a dead dog that had been torn to pieces."

"Anything else, Sergeant?" Berkstresser asked.

"Yessir. The biggest damn footprints I've ever seen were visible at three of the five homesteads. They might have been at the first two, but I wasn't looking for them. And one more thing, sir."

"Go ahead."

He pulled a handkerchief from his pocket and opened it up from the corners. They could see it was filled with hairs.

The Sergeant set them on the Captain's desk and explained, "These were found on the broken door, in one of the barns, on the dead dog and in two of the cabins. Don't sniff at them, sir. You'll regret it."

Grammy shot up out of her chair. She walked over to the desk and grabbed the handkerchief and boldly sniffed its contents. And then she looked gravely at the Captain and shook her head.

"Forest devils. They're back."

"What do you suggest?"

"Send your men out to collect all the homesteaders and bring them back here. Immediately!" she answered.

"We can't do that. We have no authority to remove people from their homes, Grammy. We're here to protect them."

"You have five dead families already. Believe me, they are no longer alive. You must do what I say. Because if you don't, my dear Captain Berkstresser, you won't have any homesteaders to protect."

Chapter 21

Epilogue

Fort Thornside was eventually abandoned in 1800. The United States made the famous Louisiana Purchase and bought the Louisiana Territory from France in 1803.

Spanish land grants were honored throughout the territory for another year. The site of the Ozark frontier settlements, associated with what later became known as the Thornside expedition, were abandoned at the same time as the fort and town were.

As to why the area ceased to be a viable area for homesteaders, settlers and an entire Army post was never sufficiently explained.

Some say that because the Army post was never commissioned by Washington, it never had a chance at longevity. Others counter that explanation with the question, even if the army had to move on, why didn't the town and the homesteaders remain?

Forest fires in that area have all but guaranteed that the old fort's exact location will never be known. Unless you pay heed to recent satellite imagery of that area that appears to show a fairly large rectangular pattern in the ground. It has yet to be investigated.

The heavy dragoons were the 2nd Regiment 1st Battalion Company C of the Georgia Horse Rangers. As explained earlier, because of their horses, they were basically a mobile infantry unit.

Here's where things get a bit interesting. Major Smythe's deployment, along with his infantry unit to the Upper Missouri Territory which is what Washington called that part of the Louisiana Territory, is well documented. Their return is as well, even noting the Major's unauthorized, but eventually approved, transfer of three cannons to the Georgia military unit.

Captain Berkstresser's deployment, along with his unit to the Upper Missouri Territory, is also well documented. The paperwork from Washington, making Berkstresser and his unit responsible for the three cannons, found its way to Georgia. This speaks to a fairly efficient accounting system, considering the times.

After that, nothing.

Berkstresser and Company C of the Georgia Horse Rangers disappear. No return to Georgia. No decommissioning. No assimilation into a larger unit. They just disappear.

Captain Sylvester Berkstresser is never mentioned again in the military archives. No promotion. No death. No discharge.

An inquiry was made in 1807 on behalf of Berkstresser's wife, Abigail. A small detachment of men was sent to the new frontier. They returned six months later to report the fort and settlement were abandoned, with no sign of the Captain or his men.

They could not find anyone who had lived in Thornside or had even tried to settle on any of the abandoned homesteads. Their report made a note of rumors concerning unfriendly beasts in the area. But they could not corroborate such a notion.

The decent thing for the military to do would have been to declare the Captain and his men deceased so that the widows could receive a stipend. But the United States government began their miserly ways early, and that simply declared them missing in action. Although, when pressed about to what action they were referring, the military went silent.

On a more personal and interesting note, Major Smythe returned home to Katherine, who was five months pregnant. Having been gone far too long to be the father, Smythe quietly divorced her, angry that it was someone else who melted her frigid demeanor.

He went on to marry Constance Belvedere, the woman who remained faithful on the frontier. They had four children and a very happy marriage. Sadly, he only made it to the rank of colonel by his retirement.

Several decades later, as the area that had been the site of Fort Dominguez and the town of Thornside became re-populated, rumors circulated. Sightings of unusual creatures that walked upright, stood seven to eight feet tall and smelled like skunks were reported. There were stories of calamitous encounters as well. They simply became part of the legend and folklore of the area.

By the end of the Civil War, the rumors had dried up. There were other real monsters to contend with, but they were human. The Red Legs and bushwhackers ran roughshod over parts of Missouri, and they were horror enough for most people.

The Ozark Forest Devils have all but been forgotten. But there was a time when they were much too real for a group of settlers who were trying to make their way in this rugged new land.

Enjoy the next in the series.

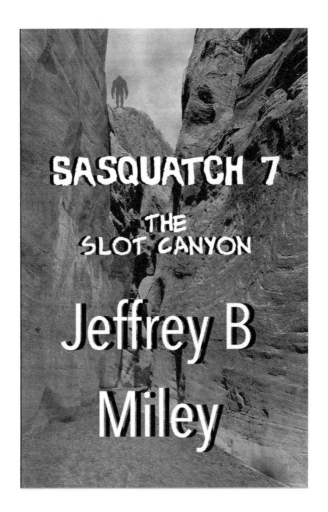

Made in the USA
Monee, IL
28 September 2024

4821fa1c-aa23-496a-8967-1042c0b7c419R01